Mat Magic at O'Mara's

The Guesthouse on the Green
Series, Book 15

Michelle Vernal

Chapter One

♥

Howth, November 2002

'Noah, we're leaving in one minute!' Roisin O'Mara bellowed up the stairs.

'I can't find Mr Nibbles, Mummy!' Noah bellowed back.

Roisin's eyes rolled heavenward. Since the move from London back to Ireland, there'd been more dramas with Stef the Gerbil, formerly known as Steve and Mr Nibbles, than on any television soap. Noah's beloved pets were not managing change well, or rather, Noah wasn't. Roisin was convinced the gerbils' recent naughtier-than-usual behaviour was an attention ploy on her son's part. She sighed, hearing him thudding about looking for his furry friend, her hand resting on the bannister and a trainer-clad foot on the bottom step, ready to thunder up the stairs and join the search. A missing gerbil she did not need on this, his first day at a new school.

The puzzle was Noah had more attention than ever now that she'd set up home here in Howth with Shay. Shay was very good with him, too. His patience was admirable. It was one of the many things she loved about him, and Noah adored him in return. Her little boy was surrounded by her ever-expanding side of the family here, too.

Mammy, for instance, only lived up the road and had called in daily to see how they were settling in. One or the other of her sisters and their offspring were also forever popping by, with the novelty of Roisin being in Ireland yet to wear off. Still, it didn't matter because the person her son was missing was his dad, and he was in the Emirates.

Colin, the arse as her sisters referred to her ex, might have freed her up to move back home to Ireland by taking a new job overseas, but it came at a cost. And she wouldn't have wished his relocating to a country over ten hours away by plane on her son for anything.

'It's alright, Mammy. I found him.'

Roisin sent up a silent thank you.

'He was sitting in the toilet roll basket again. I think it makes him feel safe.'

Roisin thought he wouldn't be safe if she caught him there. Sure, he'd given Shay's poor mammy a terrible start jumping out of the basket like so when she'd reached down for a fresh roll of paper the other day!

Noah appeared on the landing, holding his furry little pet close to his chest. At least he was dressed and had run a comb through his hair. That was something. 'Put him in his cage, now, son. We've got to be on our way.' She left him to it.

Noah's new school bag, a Spiderman splurge, was hanging in readiness for his day ahead on the hook in the hall alongside their coats. Grabbing it, Roisin entered the kitchen to grab his lunch box and drink bottle. Her eyes swept the kitchen, landing on the last of the masking taped boxes on the floor beside the Welsh Dresser. When the mover's truck pulled up outside the house she and Shay had rented because of its proximity to the local primary school, Roisin had gone into pranayama breathing overdrive. Seeing the amount of gear, they'd somehow accumulated between the three of them carted in through the front door, beginning to fill what had been an empty two-bed-roomed shell, had felt overwhelming. Now they were on top of the unpacking, and the place was starting to feel like a home, she thought with a modicum of satisfaction.

Shay was seated at his temporary workstation, the kitchen table with a half-eaten slice of toast and mug of coffee in easy reach. They planned to create a nook, a dedicated workspace, for him in the living room. He was engrossed in whatever he was tapping away at on his laptop. 'Alright?' he asked her absently.

'Lost gerbil drama averted,' Roisin replied, not expecting a reply. As she moved past Shay, his hand suddenly snaked out to pat her on the bottom. 'Cheeky!'

'I'll say.' He winked at her before focussing on the Edinburgh music festival he was working on. His official job title was Creative Producer, but he'd diversified into event management; predominantly large-scale music events. It suited him because Shay was a passionate muso, play-ing the fiddle in a Dublin pub-based band called The Sullivans, which was how he'd met Roisin.

Roisin fetched Noah's drink bottle from the fridge and then added a banana from the fruit bowl in his lunchbox, also Spiderman, before clicking it shut. She glanced out the window overlooking the garden, which was swallowed up by Noah's new trampoline. A gift from Mammy and Donal. Shay had raked the last leaves that had littered the lawn into a sodden pile, and the spindly branches from the tree responsible were visible over the neighbour's fence. So far, the threat-ened showers were holding off and hopefully would do so until Noah had been delivered into the hands of his new teacher, Miss Dunlop.

Shoving Noah's break time necessities in his bag, Roisin did a quick check, mentally ticking off the pencil case; fecking Spiderman and his never-ending accessories was costing her a bomb, she thought, locating his exercise books and ruler. He was good to go, and zipping up the bag, she slung it over her shoulder, clearing her throat with an 'ahem,' hand on hip stance in front of Shay. 'Do I look alright?' Her hair was pulled back in a ponytail, and she'd put her customary black leggings on along with a long-sleeved top made of some sporty fabric designed to wick away sweat.

Shay raised his head, and Roisin saw amusement glinting in his dark eyes as they lit up on her.

'Sure, you always look great, Rosi.'

Roisin pulled a face. 'Not true. What about the fringe?' She referenced their first date when her friend Jenny accidentally slipped with the scissors, leaving her with a look she'd rather forget.

'Okay, you always look great to me. Happy?'

Roisin nodded.

'And it's the school run, not the red carpet at the Baftas.'

'I know that, but first impressions are important, and what Mammy says is true. I need to look the part.'

'Okay, so you're asking me, do you look like a yoga teacher with a new studio people should be dying to check out?'

'Right.'

'Well, why don't you give me a demonstration of your downward dog, and I'll let you know.' Shay grinned wolfishly.

Before Roisin could think of a suitable comeback, a familiar voice from the hallway made them jump.

'I've been practising my downward dog since you told me it would help my shoulder mobility.' Maureen O'Mara hustled into the kitchen, untying the belt of her new green coat. 'If you've a minute, Rosi, you could tell me whether I'm after getting my backside high enough in the air. I don't mind telling you it's no small feat when you've Pooh sniffing about the place and Donal going on about being unable to see the television.'

'There's no time for that now, Mammy. I've got to get Noah to school.' Roisin was impatient. A visit from Mammy this morning was up there with missing gerbils.

Ignoring Roisin's statement, Maureen looked past her eldest daughter and sniffed. 'Oh, good morning to you there, Shay. I didn't see you hiding behind that screen of yours.'

'Morning, Maureen. Long time no see.'

Maureen's eyes narrowed at the tongue-in-cheek remark, and Roisin squirmed as Shay looked everywhere except at the woman who was as good as his mother-in-law these days asked. 'How're you today?'

Poor Shay struggled to make eye contact with Mammy since he'd inadvertently flashed her with a full frontal a few months back. The unfortunate incident occurred in Santorini when the family had holidayed on the Greek island for the oldest O'Mara child, Patrick's wedding. Shay hadn't known Mammy had swung by their room while he was showering and had exited the ensuite starkers.

'I'll be better once I've seen that grandson of mine off to his new school. My stomach's all in knots for him.'

'He'll be grand. Sure, he's already met his new teacher, you know that. Miss Dunlop's lovely and smiley, unlike those scary nuns you sent us to. And I told you yesterday, I'm walking Noah to school this morning. You'd no need to call by.' Roisin was beginning to rue the day she'd given her mammy a spare house key.

Maureen flapped her hand. 'Sure, you're a woman in business now, Roisin. You've not got time to be doing school runs and the like. That's what I'm here for. Your years of struggling alone in London are over now that I'm a stone's away.'

'I was married most of that time, Mammy, so I was hardly alone.'

'You might as well have been. Now you get yourself down to the studio and put the finishing touches on it before Saturday's grand opening. I'll help you once I've finished the line dancing.'

Roisin glanced at her mammy's feet. Sure enough, she'd put her cowboy boots on. With the collar of the coat Ciara from her favourite clothing boutique in Howth had told her was called wintergreen, her matching beret, and the ankle boots, she looked like a very confused spy. She looked to Shay exasperatedly, but he just smiled and shrugged.

Mammy meant well, Roisin reminded herself. She was just excited to have her and Noah living nearby. Still, and all she'd have liked a little sisterly sympathy when she'd broached Mammy's propensity for popping in when she least expected it with them.

'What did you expect? It's Mammy we're talking about,' Aisling had said while Moira unhelpfully added, 'I told you so.'

Things would settle down once the novelty wore off, Roisin had taken to reassuring herself. Or at least she hoped they would.

It wasn't easy though, especially when she felt...what? She tried to find the word, to sum up how her mam's surprise offer to loan her enough money to put a deposit down on an upstairs yoga studio here in Howth, which she'd accepted, of course, made her feel.

Beholden sprang to mind.

Chapter Two

♥

'Nana!' Noah launched himself on his nan even though he'd seen her yesterday and the day before. 'Mr Nibbles escaped, but I found him hiding with the toilet rolls in the basket again.'

Maureen was more interested in her grandson than his wayward gerbil. 'Let me get a look at you, Noah.' She held him at arm's length. 'Don't you look smart in your uniform? Doesn't he look smart?' She asked Roisin and Shay, who echoed the sentiment. 'Now, why don't you stand against the cupboard doors there? They'll make a grand backdrop, and I'll take a photograph.' Maureen dug around in her bag. 'I came prepared with my camera.'

Noah looked up at his beloved Nana, and as his hair flopped in his eye, Roisin wished she'd put her foot down for a haircut before the new term began. He was adamant, though. He wanted his hair longer like Shay's, and since Shay refused to get a number two or even three in solidarity with him, Roisin hadn't pushed it. It was only hair, after all. The little boy had bigger things to deal with, like an absent father and starting at a new school.

'I don't like this uniform as much as my old one. It's itchy.' Noah's voice quivered.

'Right,' Roisin said brusquely. 'Time we were off! Not messing about with photos, Mammy.'

Maureen bristled. 'Can a Nana not get a photo of her eldest grand-child on his first day of school?'

'I'm six, Nana, not a baby. Where's Pooh?'

Roisin picked up on the tremor in his voice and jumped in quickly, knowing she needed to get this show on the road. She didn't want to risk Noah spiralling into a meltdown and refusing to leave the house. 'It's not his first-day Mammy. It's his first day at this school, and you can take a photo at the gates.' Keeping her tone brusque, she said to Noah, 'Sure, you're a lucky boy this morning because you've me and your nana escorting you to school.'

'And Pooh,' Maureen added, catching on. 'He's waiting patiently on the front doorstep. I didn't like to bring him inside. Donal's after giving him his leftovers last night, and they were very rich. They're playing havoc with his system.'

Noah, eager to see the poodle, turned tail and raced out to the hall. Roisin, in hot pursuit, grabbed hers and Noah's coats, helping her son into his, then sliding into hers, called out a goodbye to Shay.

'Have a great day, Noah!' echoed from the kitchen, and Roisin reached for the door knob.

'Not so fast, Roisin O'Mara. I've something for you.' Maureen appeared and picked up a bulging carry bag she'd left beside the door.

'But Nana, it's not mummy's first day of school.'

'Ah, now don't be fretting, Noah. I've something for you in my bag of tricks, too.' Maureen's hand plunged into the bag. 'Here we are. One for you and one for you.'

Roisin half expected Noah to remark her present was bigger than his, given the form he was in, as she ripped off the wrapping paper to reveal pink, shiny fabric. This did not bode well, and she handed the paper to her mammy, who balled it up and stuffed it back in the bag. She unfolded it.

'A Spiderman sticker book!'

'What do you say, Noah?' Roisin said automatically as she shook out the garment, a jacket.

'Thank you, Nana.'

'You're welcome poppet. Slip it in your school bag, like. You'll be able to show all those new friends you'll be after making. Turn it over, Roisin.'

Roisin's brown eyes, carbon copies of her mam's, were round in horror as doing so, she saw the pink material had been inscribed with the logo of her new business, sort of. Instead of The Bendy Yoga Studio, a name her mammy as the majority shareholder in the studio venture had the final say in, it read The Bendy Yoga Ladies.'

'Do you get it? It's a play on words. Remember how desperate you were to be one of the Pink Ladies after you saw the Grease film? And you wouldn't let poor Aisling be part of your girl gang.'

'I do, Mammy,' Roisin attempted a smile. 'I was twelve at the time.' She didn't add that it was no longer one of her life goals.

'Do you not like it, then?'

Ah no, a wounded Mammy was the worst of them all. 'Oh no, it's grand.'

'Put it on then. Let's see what it looks like. I thought you could wear it to school like and spread the word with the mams and the dads. Smart marketing is what it's called Roisin.'

An eejitty arse in a pink jacket was more like it, Roisin thought, cringing at the thought of herself parading around at the school gates singing Look at Me, I'm Sandra Dee. She was glad Aisling wasn't here to see her get her comeuppance for not letting her join her gang all those years ago. She'd say it was karma. As for Moira, Roisin winced at what she'd have to say when she heard about this. 'Sure, it's chilly out there today, Mammy. I think I'll stick with my coat.' Roisin added a 'Brrr' for good measure.

'Tis windproof and rain resistant. You'll be warm as toast. Don't you think your mammy will look pretty in pink, Noah?'

'I don't like pink.'

Maureen ignored him as she tugged at Roisin's sleeve.

'Get off Mammy.' Roisin tried to pull away, but her mam had a tight grip on her coat.

'I think you look gorgeous in pink!' Shay called from the kitchen.

She'd deal with him later, Roisin thought, and as her mammy gave a particularly determined tug on the arm of her coat, she knew she was fighting a losing battle. If Mammy were to stand in front of the magic mirror in Snow White and ask, 'Mirror, Mirror, who's the most determined of them all,' it would reply, 'You are Maureen, with Moira running a close second.' As such, Roisin shrugged out of her coat and draped it on the hook before letting Mammy help her into her new jacket.

'There we go. You look a picture, Roisin. Give me a twirl.'

Roisin obliged, feeling a complete arse.

'I've another surprise for you.' Maureen reached into the depths of her carry bag and produced a second matching jacket. 'I've one too. So have Aisling and Moira. I'm only giving you yours first because it's your studio. I thought about sending one to Cindy because, technically, she's my daughter now that she's married to Patrick. I've got to be careful she doesn't feel left out, but you know yourself she's not going to be drumming much business up over there in Los Angeles.'

Before Roisin could mutter, a Jaysus wept; her mam had whipped off her coat and donned her matching pink jacket.

No, no! Roisin cried silently, spying the polka-dot neck scarf hidden under her mam's coat.

Maureen struck a pose. 'It's important to look the part, Rosi.'

It could have been worse. Mammy could have gone for the skin-tight trousers Olivia Newton-John wore. Instead, she'd opted for her Mo-pants, as she called the market knock-off stretchy leggings, Roisin favoured for yoga. Never one to miss an opportunity when friends had asked her where she'd sourced her comfortable pants from, she'd had Roisin bring in a load fresh off the London markets, rebranding them to the Mo-pant, short for Maureen.

The Mo-pant was an iconic brand amongst women of a certain age around Howth.

They were officially twinning.

Noah opened the door, 'Mummy, Nana, come on, or we'll be late.'

He was right, Roisin thought, herding her mam out the door.

'Remember, shoulders back, Rosi, don't be slouching. You want everyone to be able to read your jacket logo now. Free advertising is what it is.'

Roisin thought the walk of shame is what it is, closing the door behind them.

Chapter Three

♥

'That will teach them. Eyes on the road when you're driving.' Maureen tutted at the passing car as its brakes squealed in a narrowly missed collision at the end of the road.

They were making a holy show of themselves. The fecking pink jackets had a lot to answer for, Roisin thought, watching Noah skipping ahead with Pooh, the lead in his hand. To be fair to Mammy, bringing Pooh along for the school run was a smart move. Her temperamental poodle was proving to be the perfect distraction from first-day nerves for Noah.

A little boy in the same uniform as Noah and maybe a year or two older opened his front gate and fell in alongside her son. She smiled as the lull in the morning traffic allowed her to catch snippets of their mostly one-sided conversation as Noah told him about Pooh and his habit of letting off.

'Ah, now there's a sight that would warm your heart. Look at the wee dotes,' Maureen said with a nod in her grandson and his new friend's direction. 'Pooh's a grand icebreaker, so he is.'

Roisin couldn't argue with that and was more inclined to link her arm through her mam's.

It was a gesture which made Maureen smile and give her daughter's arm a squeeze of acknowledgement. 'The line dancing ladies are all green over me having a daughter and grandson so close by.'

'Well, Shay and I appreciate all the help you and Donal have given us.' Donal had found the house they'd rented and had a word with the landlord on their behalf, and Mammy had kept them fed and watered while they got settled in. Then, there was the studio, of course.

Initially, Roisin thought she might consider hiring a room at the local community centre. However, Mammy had kept her ear to the ground, and when Rosemary Farrell had mentioned she, too, was going to have a live-in manfriend and that Cathal Carrick the Cobbler would be shacking up with her, she'd had one of her epiphanies. Why didn't Roisin utilise the flat above Cathal's shoe shop for her studio?

Mammy had set to work on Cathal negotiating a discounted rent. Once he'd moved his furniture out, Roisin was left with a perfectly workable space for her studio if she knocked a wall down and incorporated what had been his bedroom into the living room. The wall wasn't load-bearing, and Cathal agreed she could remove it by adding a clause in the lease. If Roisin wanted to break their rental arrangement early, she'd have to replace it. Roisin had signed on the dotted line and the flat was hers for the next two years.

'It's a shame the Dublin Marathon's been and gone,' Maureen intruded on her thoughts.

'I don't think Aisling and Moira would agree with you. They'd had enough of the constant wintergreen pong.'

'This season's hottest colour.'

Roisin and her sisters had discussed Ciara with a 'C' who worked in a boutique on Howth's main road and whom their mam treated as her personal fashion guru, asserting that wintergreen was in vogue. They were doubtful it was a colour, but Mammy was adamant that her new spy coat wasn't simply green. It was winter green. 'It was the smelly ingredient in Deep Heat before it was this season's hottest colour, Mammy.'

'Don't be talking to me about the Deep Heat, Roisin. I know what happens when my son-in-laws' apply it, forget to wash their hands, and then go to the toilet. Thank you very much. And I've no wish to be reminded of it this early in the morning. As I said, it's a shame the marathon's been because it's a missed marketing opportunity. Quinn and Tom could have done their part by wearing singlets with the Bendy Yoga Lads on the back.'

Roisin doubted Quinn and Tom would see it as a shame. Besides, their marathon days were over because her sisters had barred them from entering next year's event. They'd had enough of the running commentary on the pulled muscles and hearing about the Deep Heat burn.

Maureen suddenly stopped; head cocked to the side. 'My phone's after ringing.' She delved into her bag.

All the O'Mara women were on high alert because Patrick and Cindy's baby was due any day now, but they needed to get Noah to school. 'Mammy, the whole point of the mobile phone is that you can be mobile. You can walk and talk at the same time,' Roisin said, watching her stab at buttons blindly. 'Give it here.'

Maureen passed it over.

'Hello, Maureen O'Mara's phone.'

'It's your brother Patrick, Moira.'

'It's Roisin, Pat. It's Noah's first day at his new school, and we're after walking him there now, so we can't talk long. How's Cindy?'

'Give me the phone, Roisin.' Maureen grabbed it, but Roisin turned away.

'Oh, poor you. Okay, I'll pass it on to Mammy. Bye now.'

Maureen glowered at her daughter as she handed her phone back. 'Well? What's the news?'

'No news. Cindy's very well, but he's worn out.' This was typical of her brother. He was the biggest drama queen of them all.

'Poor Patrick. It's very stressful being a daddy-to-be,' Maureen stated loyally. 'And a Nana in waiting for the fifth time. I don't know how my poor heart takes it. Donal's taken to pacing, and we've had our bags packed for a week now.'

Mammy and Donal would fly to Los Angeles when the baby was born. As much as Roisin couldn't have done without their help this last while, it would be nice to wave them off for a few weeks. Not only that. She was looking forward to becoming an aunt again. Her hand strayed to her middle as they walked along. Her monthly had arrived bang on time last week, but it was the early days of the baby-making stakes. Some might think she was mad contemplating a baby when she was determined to succeed in her new business venture. Still, not everyone had the sort of family support she was lucky to have. The set-up above Carrick's the Cobblers meant she'd be able to have the baby there with her, and she knew Shay's mam would be hands on and, of course, it went without saying, Mammy would be too. Right now, though, it was Cindy's turn.

They rounded the corner to see children being disgorged from the line of cars. It was the usual school gate chaos, and Roisin was glad they lived within walking distance. She had no car yet, but Donal was on to it and determined to find her a bargain.

'Pooh!' Noah suddenly shrieked as the lead slipped from his hand. The poodle bounded toward a fluffy, white cockapoo prancing about at the heels of a woman whose short, curly hairstyle closely resembled her dog's. The woman was too busy waving at a pig-tailed little girl to notice her wee dog's approaching paramour.

Time seemed to slow down, like at the end of a film where the hero is reunited with his sweetheart as Maureen and Roisin saw the poodle begin yapping at the dainty dog with her smart red collar. If she had eyelashes, she'd be batting them, Roisin thought, amused.

'Come on, Nancy,' the cockapoo's owner tugged the lead.

Pooh, seeming to realise he was about to lose his new friend, decided there was no time for subtle flirtation and, without warning, went straight to the main course and mounted his new friend.

Nancy's owner shrieked, 'Get off her, you dirty boy.'

Roisin cringed as heads turned to see what the shouting was all about. This was not how she'd envisaged Noah's arrival at his new primary school. Somewhere, an excited child's voice shouted, 'The big dogs after sexing the little one!' There was always one know-it-all when it came to the facts of life, Roisin thought, recalling how Carmel O'Shaughnessy charged them all ten pence for a peek at the Karma Sutra book she'd found hidden under her mam and dad's bed. Roisin had been adamant her mammy and daddy didn't do that sort of thing, and she'd been a product of immaculate conception.

'It's alright.' Maureen approached the scene with her hands raised in an 'I come in peace' manner. 'He's been seen too. Sure you know yourself, old habits die hard.'

'Get your dog off, Nancy!'

Mammy wouldn't take kindly to the woman's tone; Roisin thought anxious things would go from bad to worse. Indeed, her mam's lips had flatlined, and her eyes narrowed. Mercifully, she said, 'Pooh, c'mere to me now!'

Pooh was oblivious as he joyfully went through the motions, recalling his glory days. Then, a collective gasp whipped through the crowd as something sleek and black flew through the air and stealth-bombed the pair.

Was it a panther? No, get a grip, Roisin told herself, her hand on her heart. Sure, it was a black lab, and he was none too happy with Pooh as he emitted a low growl and stalked around the amorous pair. Pooh paused long enough to bare his poodley teeth.

'George!' A tracksuit-clad man with a head on him that would make an onion cry elbowed his way through the gathering crowd of parents and children. The labrador's eyes seemed to glow and were pinned on Pooh.

'Nana, save Pooh!' Noah cried.

Pooh, aware he had competition, bared his teeth and growled back at the interloper, finally dismounting Nancy, who was swooped up into the arms of her traumatised owner.

Without warning, the two dogs sprang at one another, snapping and snarling.

'George!'

'Pooh!' Maureen and the onion head man began dancing about the dogs like prize fighters as they looked for an in to drag their pooches away.

A group of ruffian children had formed a semi-circle and shouted, 'Fight, fight, fight.' While mams and dads attempted to shield the eyes of their more delicate offspring. Then, help arrived in the shape of a woman toting a green plastic bucket from which water sloshed. Roisin recognised her as Miss Dunlop, Noah's new teacher.

As icy water landed on the warring dogs, and their owners they yelped and sprang apart. Pooh skulked to Maureen's side, and George hid behind the onion-headed man's legs.

'The show's over.' Miss Dunlop announced as a bell pealed, and children stampeded through the gates.

'Good morning, Noah,' The primly dressed woman of middling years said before nodding in Roisin's direction.

'Good morning, Miss Dunlop.' Noah, awestruck, took the outstretched hand of his new teacher and, without so much as a backward glance at his mammy or nana, trotted alongside her toward the classrooms.

Pulling her sodden jacket from her, Maureen remarked, 'His new teacher's very efficient.'

'Miss Dunlop's great. Scary but great, and the kids love her,' a voice from behind said.

Roisin turned to see a woman around her own age standing there. Unlike herself, though, she was dressed smartly in a white shirt and pin-striped trousers visible thanks to an open camel-coloured coat. Roisin instantly coveted her jacket. Blondes always looked so elegant in camel.

'You're new to the area, I take it?' Light danced in the stranger's blue eyes, hinting at a sense of humour.

'How did you know?' Roisin grimaced.

The woman dimpled, 'A lucky guess.'

Roisin found herself instantly warming to her as she introduced herself. 'I'm Roisin, and yes, my son and I moved home from London a few weeks ago.'

'I'm Becca. It's nice to meet you. I take it you're behind the yoga studio opening?' Becca gestured toward Roisin's pink jacket.

'My mam's idea.'

'I think they're great.'

'See Roisin, I told you. Smart marketing. I'm Maureen O'Mara, Roisin's mammy.' Maureen looked up from where she'd stooped down to tell Pooh he was a naughty boy.

'Nice to meet you, Maureen. You don't happen to go to the line dancing now, do you?'

Maureen straightened, before performing a side shuffle and pivot turn as confirmation.

'I thought so. The cowboy boots gave it away. My mam, Peg, goes too. She takes it very seriously, like.'

'Oh, I know Peg. I can see the resemblance now, so I can. She's very good at the Watermelon Crawl.' Maureen began humming a tune and doing some more fancy footwork.

Roisin and Becca exchanged the complicit smiles of women, sensing they were kindred spirits.

'I've already registered for your nine-thirty class on a Thursday,' Becca was saying, but Roisin looked past her to where the onion-headed man and curly-haired cockapoo woman were glaring at them. If looks could kill.

Becca tracked her gaze. 'Oh, don't be worrying about those two. Dean's a dentist, but honest to God, the breath on him would make yer eyes water. And Philomena is a pain in the arse. She heads up the Parent's Association and is forever after fundraising.'

Excellent, Roisin thought. She'd gotten on the wrong side of the Parents' Association head honcho on the first day of school. Her tongue flicked to the molar that had been bothering her, and she made a note to steer clear of any dentist in Howth called Dean.

'Roisin, we need to shake a leg, or I'll be coming down with pneumonia if I don't get home and change out of these wet things. Will we see you at the Bendy Yoga's grand opening then, Becca?'

'You will, Maureen.'

Roisin smiled. 'It was nice meeting you, Becca.' The morning hadn't been all bad, she decided, because she had the feeling she'd made her first friend here in Howth.

Chapter Four

♥

It was bedlam on the top floor in the family quarters of O'Mara's Guesthouse. Given the apartment was home to four adults and three children under three, this was par for the course.

Aisling and Moira O'Mara had grown up above the guesthouse opposite St Stephen's Green in a long row of Georgian buildings. These days, the sisters might reside in identical bedrooms from their childhood, but they'd added to the mix. Aisling, who managed the guesthouse, was married to Quinn, owner of Quinn's Bistro and had five-month-old twins. At the same time, Moira and her partner Tom, both students, were parents to the toddler, Kiera. Somehow, they muddled together for what they all agreed was not a permanent arrangement but one that worked for them financially and practically.

Kiera, who would spend the morning with her Nana Sylvia, was in no mood to be hurried along. Moira had other ideas, given she was due at the college where she was an art student in half an hour. Kiera was staging a sit-in on the kitchen floor demanding more Cheerios. A frazzled Moira did her best to explain to her daughter the cereal box was empty because she'd eaten it all for breakfast. She had a good appetite did Kiera. Tom, a doctor in training, stumbled in on the drama yawning, hair mussed and pyjamas on, a concession Moira said he had to make given their shared living arrangements. He supplemented their income by waiting tables at Quinn's Bistro, and it had been late when he'd finally fallen into bed last night.

'I saw your tonsils then Tom.' Aisling referenced his yawn as she jiggled a disgruntled Connor on her hip. His twin sister, Aoife, happily practised rolling onto her tummy and flipping onto her back under the baby gym. Aisling had known the sort of day she was in for when Connor had woken her, wailing at five am. At just over five months, her son was an early teether. Aoife, thank goodness, was not showing any signs just yet.

'Sorry,' Tom muttered. 'There was a group at the restaurant last night that wouldn't take the hint and go home.' He yawned again but covered his mouth this time.

Unlike her husband, Tom was an early riser no matter when his head hit the pillow. Quinn was still snoring when she'd last popped her head in their bedroom. His ability to sleep through the morning chaos never ceased to amaze her.

Moira scooped her protesting daughter up and thrust her at her daddy. 'Tom, your mam will be here in half an hour. She's taking Kiera to the zoo today, although I'm not sure why, given we live in one. Be sure to bundle her up. It's going to be freezing.' She planted a kiss on his cheek. 'Right. I've got to go.' Then, picking up her art satchel, she legged it out the door.

Hearing the door bang shut, Aisling envied her little sister but felt terrible because Connor wasn't carrying on for no good reason. The poor dote. She'd no excuse to head out the door and downstairs to the hub of the guesthouse, the reception area, for a reprieve. Not when Freya – O'Mara's assistant manager, was proving more than capable. Sure, she'd pop down later. Bronagh, Freya, Ita and Mrs Flaherty loved fussing over the babies. Then, seeing Tom bleary-eyed, talking of elephants and tigers and all the things Kiera would see at the zoo with her nan felt a dart of sympathy. The poor sod was still half asleep. 'There's tea in the pot, Tom. Sure, you look like you need a brew.'

'Thanks Ash. I do.'

Kiera was now sufficiently amped about her outing, and wriggling free from her daddy, she toddled over on two plump legs to see what Aoife was up to.

The phone bursting into life seemed to startle Connor out of his grump, and his sore gums were forgotten as he began beaming and cooing. Aisling cuddled him to her as Tom answered, and, hearing him greet Bronagh, she set Connor down on the mat next to his sister. Kiera had lost interest in her cousin and was flinging toys out of the basket a safe distance away.

Tom passed the phone over, and Aisling said good morning to the trusty receptionist, who was as much a part of the guesthouse as the O'Mara family.

'Morning Bronagh.'

'Good morning, Aisling. If you've got a minute, we could do with you having a word with Mrs Flaherty before she goes home. She's had a face on her like a slapped arse all morning.'

Aisling sighed. 'Oh dear. Has Mr Fox paid the bin a visit?' The cook's nemesis was the little red fox who lived in the Iveagh Gardens behind the guesthouse. Under cover of darkness, Foxy Loxy, as Moira had nicknamed him, would dig under the brick wall separating the gardens from the guesthouse courtyard to raid the bin for tasty breakfast scraps. Many times, Mrs Flaherty threatened to end him with the rolling pin and other choice phrases when confronted with evidence of his visit scattered about the courtyard. Mercifully, she'd yet to have an up close and personal encounter with the fox because all the sisters were fond of their nocturnal guest.

'He has, but you know we've also a posh London couple staying who checked in yesterday?'

'The pipe-cleaners,' Roisin spoke her thoughts aloud.

'You'd be right there. The Burton-Harris's and I've seen more fat on a hen's kneecap. They're very rude and sniffy the pair of them. You know, the sort with the silver spoon wedged up their—'

'I know the sort,' Aisling interrupted.

'Well, they're here for his uncle's funeral, and they were sure to tell me his aunt was responsible for booking them into the guesthouse because they'd have opted for the Shelbourne.'

'Charming.' Aisling liked to give their guests the benefit of the doubt. She'd tell herself you never knew what was going on in a person's life when dealing with their more unpleasant guests. 'Still and all, they're grieving.'

'They also asked me to let the cook know they were gluten intolerant and vegetarian. And you know how Mrs Flaherty is about that sort of thing. I don't have it in me to tell her, Aisling.'

Aisling did know how Mrs Flaherty felt about food intolerances and vegetarianism. They were up there with how she felt about poor old Foxy Loxy raiding the bin. 'Do you want me to come down and speak with her? Tell her myself, like?' She kept one eye on Kiera, chatting to the conductor of the most annoying toy ever, her plastic musical Wheels on the Bus. Aoife was now smacking the swinging object on the baby gym, and Connor was watching her raptly. Tom meanwhile looked as though he were on a Barry's tea commercial as he said, 'Aah, now that's better,' swallowing a mouthful of the brew.

'I wouldn't normally ask you to Aisling, but you've a way with her, and Mrs Flaherty wasn't herself last week either. I asked her what was ailing her, but she was a closed book. Perhaps Mr Flaherty's not been wearing his snoring headgear again, and he's giving her sleepless nights?'

'Hmm, perhaps.'

'The thing is, Aisling, I'm worried that on top of the fox to-do first thing, she'll bop one of the London duo with the frying pain when they finally come down for breakfast and place their order.'

Aisling knew Bronagh was only half joking. 'Right-ho. I'll be down in a few ticks.'

'Dramas?' Tom asked over the top of his mug.

'Potential dramas,' Aisling confirmed going in search of her Christian Louboutin boots. The low heel was a compromise she'd made for the sake of her children. Then, checking she'd not got milk stains or vomit patches on her top, she picked up her babies. One for each hip.

'I can watch them if you like?' Tom offered half-heartedly because that was the sort of bloke he was.

'No, you're grand, but thanks Tom. You get yourself some breakfast. Bronagh, Freya and Ita will take these two off me as soon as I get downstairs.'

'Me!' Kiera, realising she wasn't coming, tossed the conductor aside, arms reaching out for her Aunty Aisling as she stampeded toward her.

'No. Kiera, you're staying here with me. Remember Nana's coming soon to take you to the zoo. Daddy's got to get you washed and dressed.'

'No zoo!' The bottom lip wobbled ominously, and a sob escaped.

'Sorry,' Aisling mouthed at Tom, who shrugged and trumpeted like an elephant.

'Ring Mammy and Donal. I don't think your elephant's going to work. It's an Islands in the Stream morning you're after having there, Tom.'

He paused in the trumpeting. 'I think you're right.'

Aisling left him swinging his arm like a trunk as he got up to fetch the phone. The Dolly-Kenny duet sang by her beloved Nana and Poppa D would soon dry up her niece's tears. It worked every time. Right now, she'd a temperamental breakfast cook to deal with and two babies to deliver to their honorary aunties.

Chapter Five

'**G**ood morning Ita,' Aisling sang over the droning vacuum cleaner. Ita, the guesthouse's self-titled Director of Housekeeping, looked up from where she was wearing the hallway carpet out and, seeing Aisling with a twin on either hip, quickly turned the machine off and downed tools. She made a beeline for the babies and as she clucked over Aoife and Connor, Aisling thought it might be nice if someone occasionally fussed over her, saying things like, 'Haven't you got the sweetest chubby cheeks, or look at that little tum tum.' After all, they got them both from her and the fluff of reddish-blonde hair they sported.

The lemon scent of Pledge was in the air, and Aisling's practised eye swept over the bannister rail, which gleamed thanks to Ita's efforts. It was hard to believe Moira used to call her Idle Ita due to her propensity to do as little as possible about the place. Ita had turned over a new leaf when she met her fella and began her part-time veterinary assistant course. Aisling mused that love and future prospects could work motivational wonders, aware they'd lose Ita next year when she graduated. Ah well, she'd cross that bridge when she came to it.

'I'm on my way downstairs to see Mrs Flaherty, Ita. Bronagh's after telling me she's not in good humour.'

Ita, holding Connor's pudgy little hand, pulled a face. 'She's been terrible moody for days, Aisling. I give her a wide berth because I don't trust her with that rolling pin of hers.'

Aisling laughed, although, thinking about it, she didn't either.

The door to Room Six opened, and an accent that could cut glass rang out, 'Sienna, it's a funeral we're going to, not a Hello Magazine photoshoot. Would you put the mirror down? Nothing has changed in the past five seconds.'

A pale, thirtyish rake in a black suit emerged from the room, followed by a glamorous twig clad in black with a mane of highlighted brunette hair and enormous sticky red lips.

Aisling took an educated guess that this was the gluten-intolerant, vegetarian couple she was to forewarn Mrs Flaherty about. Right, she thought, mentally rolling her sleeves up. She'd win them over with a spot of blarney, and she gave them her best smile as the couple stalked toward the stairs.

'Good morning to you. I'm Aisling O'Mara, the guesthouse manager, and this is Ita, our Director of Housekeeping. Oh, and these two,' she jiggled Aoife and Connor jollily, 'are my babbies, Aoife and Connor.'

Connor threw up on his bib, and Ita was quick off the mark to wipe his mouth and remove it. 'Sorry about that. He's teething. He brings everything up. I hope you had a comfortable night's sleep?'

The twig kept a wary distance from the babies as though they might carry a nasty contagious disease. Her lip curled as she sniffed. 'Since you ask, we were woken by a terrible ruckus just after one in the morning, as it happens. Weren't we, Ralph?'

'It sounded like a bin being turned over.' Ralph affirmed, pushing his foppish fringe out of his eyes and sniffing.

'Ah, well, now that would be the little red fox who likes to visit us now and again. I'll have a word with him about waking you up.' Aisling winked, but she was getting the feeling her Irish charm offensive was water off a duck's back. She reminded herself to give them the benefit of the doubt because the couple's unpleasantness could be down to profound grief over Ralph's uncle's passing. For all she knew, his uncle might have been like a father figure to him, and today he would say goodbye. If he didn't want to indulge in toast, or perhaps it was the meat he wasn't keen on, for breakfast, then so be it. Her job was to ensure their guests left O'Mara's happy.

'Come on, Sienna,' Ralph said, pushing past the two women. We'd better have a spot of breakfast before we call the taxi. It's going to be a long day. I wish the old git had popped his clogs in the summer. It's bound to be freezing at the do back at Aunt Jocelyn's mausoleum.'

Then again, some people were simply what they seemed. Unpleasant, Aisling thought. 'Well, you're sure to get a good breakfast to set you up for the day at O'Mara's' she called after them. Then, turned and grimaced at Ita, whispering, 'That pair will push Mrs Flaherty's buttons alright. Best I get downstairs and see to them myself,' she said before trailing down the stairs a safe distance behind them. Her nose twitched, catching a tantalising waft of bacon drifting up the stairs from the basement kitchen and dining area. She could hear the phone ringing in reception ahead of her and the clatter of cutlery in the dining room below. She'd two babbies to offload before she tackled Ralph and Sienna's breakfast order.

Bronagh had answered the call and was busy scribbling on the message pad when Aisling and her two appendages appeared. Her face was hidden by a shoulder-length curtain of jet-black hair. Aisling deduced that she'd had her roots done, which most likely meant her Liverpool-based beau Leonard Walsh and long-time guest of O'Mara's was over for the weekend. Of course, these days, he stayed with Bronagh and her mammy. It was high time Leonard and Bronagh made their arrangement permanent, Aisling thought because they made one another happy. They both deserved as much of that as they could get. For some reason, Beyonce's 'Single Ladies (Put a Ring on it)' pushed play in her head. She'd had a hand in getting the pair of them together. Perhaps it was time she had a hand in Bronagh and Lennie, as their receptionist called him, taking things to the next level.

Her eyes were itching and her nose tingling as she tried to ward off a sneeze, which put an end to pondering over just how she'd manage that. Those ornamental lilies in the vase on top of the front desk, which Bronagh was sitting at, were gorgeous, as was their smell. The Arpège scented air freshener they were competing with, not so much. Mammy was a fan favourite of the stuff and insisted on buying the cans in bulk for the guesthouse. Someone had gone to town with it this morning. Jaysus, her nose wrinkled. It was worse than when Quinn or Tom had their morning visits.

'We look forward to seeing you on the fifteenth Mr Sotheby. Goodbye now.' Bronagh put the phone down and swivelled in her chair, her eyes lighting up as she spied the twins.

Aisling frowned. 'Why've you one cheek all puffed up like so? You look like a squirrel hoarding nuts on one side of your face only.'

Bronagh looked shifty, and Aisling spied the crumbs littering the front of her blouse. 'The phone rang as I was halfway through a custard cream.' She hastily rearranged the contents of her mouth, chewing and swallowing.

'Well, I need fortification, what with the breastfeeding and having to get to the bottom of what's upsetting Mrs Flaherty. So hand one over, please.' Aisling opened her mouth like a baby bird waiting for the mammy bird to drop a worm in.

'Just the one mind.' Bronagh begrudgingly slid a drawer open and rustled about in her not-so-secret stash before shoving the biscuit in Aisling's gob.

Aisling thought it was harder to fit the whole thing in her mouth than she'd anticipated as Freya appeared from the guest's lounge with an empty box of teabags in her hand.

'We've had a run on the Earl Grey of late. I can't stand the stuff, personally speaking. It's like drinking perfume. Give me a cup of Barry's any day,' she said, putting the empty box down on the reception desk.

'Who cut your hands off then?' Bronagh muttered, picking it up and tossing it in the bin beneath her desk.

Freya paid her no heed as her eyes lit up just as Bronagh's had at the sight of Aoife and Connor.

Bronagh swiftly held her arms out. 'Give the babbies to their Aunty Bronagh, Aisling.'

'You don't need both of them, Bronagh,' Freya huffed, reaching out.

Honestly, it was just as well she'd two to go around, or there'd be ructions. Aisling thought, frantically chewing and swallowing the custardy biscuit before handing her daughter to Freya. Bronagh lucked out, she thought, feeling a smelly warmth fill Connor's nappy as she passed him over. Ah, well, she knew where the spare nappies were kept. 'You might need to respray the Arpège.'

'I told Bronagh not to be so heavy-handed,' Freya said, kissing Aoife's cheek and leaving a pinkish lipstick tattoo behind.

'If yer man in Room 3 used deodorant, I wouldn't have to be,' Bronagh shot back. 'Has he done what I think he's done?' She patted around Connor's backside.

'He has, and I'll have to leave you to sort it because the fussy food couple are after heading downstairs for breakfast. When it comes to the babbies, you've to take the good with the bad, Bronagh.'

'It's just as well you're such a wee dote then, isn't it? Because your Aunty Bronagh wouldn't do this for anyone other than you or your sister. No, she wouldn't.'

Aisling looked back over her shoulder. 'I wouldn't be jigging him too much there, Bronagh. He's after bringing up his milk not so long ago, and you'll only be spreading the you know what everywhere.'

Bronagh stopped jiggling about, which was just as well because Aisling could see the seams of her skirt straining with each knee jerk. 'Oh, I just remembered. Freya, before Aisling disappears, tell her what you're after telling me about your cousin's mammy's friend who lost ten pounds in a week.'

'Well, she was nil by mouth in hospital then.'

'You didn't mention that.'

'I didn't get the chance. The phone was after ringing.'

Aisling left them to it.

She had a temperamental cook who she happened to be very fond of to be sorting.

Chapter Six

♥

Mrs Flaherty was viciously cracking an egg against the side of the frying pan when Aisling entered her sacred domain, the kitchen. The smell of rashers frying made her stomach rumble, and it was comforting to know she'd have a rasher sandwich pressed into her hands before long. Mrs Flaherty was one of life's feeders, and as Aisling was one of life's eaters, they'd always had a good relationship. 'Good morning, Mrs Flaherty,' she said brightly.

The rotund little woman with rosy apple cheeks who looked exactly like Mother Hubbard in the nursery rhyme book Aisling had loved as a child looked up from the bowl, broken eggshell in her hand and said, 'Feck.'

Oh dear, Aisling thought.

'I've shell in the egg. I never get shell in the egg.'

'Never mind, I'll pick it out for you,' Aisling volunteered only to have her hand slapped away.

'No, get away with yer. I can manage.'

The cook's sharp tone wasn't often directed at Aisling, and she took a step back from the cooker top.

'If you want to help Aisling, then you can start by sorting the mess that fecking fox has left behind.'

That was the thing about Mrs Flaherty. Her appearance was at odds with the gob on her. The cook's heart, however, was pure gold, and Aisling didn't like to see her riled. So, eager to smooth the cook's ruffled feathers, she fetched a new pair of Marigolds from the cupboard under the sink. She slipped the yellow rubber gloves on, snapping them like a surgeon heading into the theatre to show Mrs Flaherty she meant business. Then, ducked her head out the backdoor, bracing against the November chill.

No wonder poor Mrs Flaherty was in such a spin.

Aisling's eyes raked over the trail of litter spewed across the damp courtyard. Thanks to Mr Fox's efforts, the bin was upturned, the lid he'd nosed off, half a foot away from the evidence of his crime. No wonder the noise had woken the posh pipe cleaner couple. Her gaze settled on the dug-out hole beneath the brick wall where the culprit had entered. It was no good filling it in because he'd only dig through again. Besides, her softer side argued the poor animal had to eat, and there were scraps of rind and half-eaten sausages to be had in that bin. Fine dining for foxes.

It was freezing out here, and the damp morning air would be murder on her hair, Aisling thought, shivering. As such, she got stuck in righting the bin and then, holding her breath, scooped the rubbish back into it.

Job done, she ventured back into the kitchen where Mrs Flaherty was plating a full Irish and swirling scrambled eggs around a pan. The woman took multi-tasking to the next level, Aisling thought, getting rid of the gloves. She whipped the frilly white pinny off the back of the door and slipped it over her head. Then, knotting it at the back, said, 'I'll take that through for you if you like Mrs Flaherty.'

'Where are your babbies?' Mrs Flaherty's tone suggested Aisling had abandoned them on the mean streets of Dublin town.

'To be honest with you, Mrs Flaherty, I needed a breather from the twins, so I've left them with Freya and Bronagh for half an hour, and I want to be useful, so here I am. Besides, I miss mixing and mingling with the guests.' It was a half-fib, half-truth. She did miss her morning banter with their guests. Accordingly, Aisling held her upturned palm out for the plate laden with black pudding, white pudding, sausages, bacon, beans and eggs, and two triangles of toast arranged on the side. Mrs Flaherty ignored her, swiftly scooping the creamy scrambled eggs onto the other plate's waiting toast.

'I'm perfectly able to carry a couple of breakfasts through to our guests, Aisling. It's what I'm paid for.' To prove her point, the cook picked up the plates, holding onto them with a white-knuckled grip.

Bronagh and Ita were right, Aisling thought. Mrs Flaherty was out of sorts, but she knew from experience that flattery usually worked a treat. 'And sure, I don't know what we'd do with you out, Mrs Flaherty. You could plate a fry up and present it to our guests blindfolded so you could. It's just nice to show my face with the guests now and again. I'm only on unofficial maternity leave, after all. I like to keep my finger in, so to speak.' Or, should that have been hand? Aisling wondered. Either way, her words had the desired effect, and Mrs Flaherty grudgingly relinquished the oven-warmed plates to Aisling.

'The full Irish is for the Frenchman in Room 4, and his wife is after having the scrambled eggs. And I hope you weren't thinking of skulking back upstairs without bringing the babbies down to see me? Or eating a rasher sandwich. You must keep up your strength, feeding two Aisling.'

That was more like it! 'I wouldn't dream of not bringing Aoife and Connor down to see you, Mrs Flaherty, and as it happens, I'm starving. A rasher sambo will go down very nicely.' Aisling smiled as she was shooed out the door with a, 'Would you get a move on, or the poor man's breakfast will be stone cold.'

The dining room walls at O'Mara's were lined with black and white prints of Dublin of old; the tables covered with starched white cloths. If you sat near the windows, guests got a bird's eye view through the wrought iron railings to the footpath outside. Aisling glimpsed feet in sturdy shoes splashing through puddles before scanning the half-full room for an elegant couple because, in her experience, that could be counted on when it came to their French guests. A-ha, she thought, making her way toward a man and woman who fit the bill. They were clad suitably for a damp Dublin day's sight-seeing, somehow managing that delicate balance between style and practicality. And, the woman had hair that wouldn't dare frizz! definitely French, she thought, beaming a 'Bonjour' at them. Her token effort at French was received with smiles, and she set the heaving plates down.

'Merci,' the man replied while the woman clapped her hands together at the sight of the food with an 'Oh lá lá!'

French women existing on coffee, croissants, teeny tiny slivers of brie and cigarettes was a myth then, Aisling thought, rustling up her schoolgirl French to say 'De rien'(you're welcome), adding a 'Bon appétit' for good measure. Then, seeing the suit-clad businessman behind them get up from his table, Aisling left them to enjoy breakfast.

'How was your breakfast, Sir?' She enquired, beginning to stack the cup and saucer on the all-but-licked-clean plate.

'Very good, thank you. My compliments to the cook.'

'I'll be sure to pass that on.' That, along with the 'Oh lá lá!' was sure to help restore Mrs Flaherty's good humour. Aisling risked a glance from under her lashes to the table where the posh pipe cleaners had their noses buried in the menu. She decided to give them a little longer as she balled up the serviette and tottered back toward the kitchen.

The smartly dressed woman absentmindedly forking up eggs and simultaneously scribbling notes in her open filo fax missed Aisling's smile as she passed by her table. Two men, so similar in appearance they had to be brothers, were sipping coffee at the adjacent table, and her greeting was reciprocated.

'How are those beautiful twins of yours this morning, Aisling?' A familiar voice enquired.

'Oh, good morning to you, Mrs Carmody.' Aisling paused. 'I didn't see you hiding behind your menu there.' Aisling was fond of the sweet elderly lady from Adare, who stayed with them for two days each November on her annual Christmas shopping trip to Dublin. 'They're very well, thank you. Although Connor's started early with the teething, poor wee man.'

'Well now, Aisling, don't be wasting your money on any of those fancy teething yokes. You want to steep a teaspoon of cloves in boiling water, and when it's cooled, put a few drops in his mouth. It worked a treat on my babbies, and I'd seven of them!' Her sharp blue eyes twinkled.

'I'd say that makes you an expert then, Mrs Carmody,' Aisling smiled. 'Thanks a million. I'll give it a go.' Before enquiring which department store their regular guest would be visiting today, she heard a clicking sound. Her back stiffened. Surely those weren't clicking fingers trying to get her attention? The exaggerated throat clearing that swiftly followed confirmed they were. Aisling deliberately ignored whoever it was, suspecting Ralph, the vegetarian pipe cleaner, was the culprit as she asked Mrs Carmody what she fancied for her breakfast.

The wily woman winked at Aisling. She was happy to play the game and took her time deciding on a full Irish, even though it was what she chose every morning while staying here at O'Mara's. Aisling had often wondered where she put it because she was a tiny-bird-like woman.

However, Mrs Carmody would mop her plate clean with her toast, claiming it would set her up until tea time. She was, of course, a firm favourite with Mrs Flaherty. Order taken, Aisling turned slowly to see a peeved-looking Ralph peering out from under his fringe while Sienna's expression was that of someone who'd been shat on by a pigeon.

'I'll be with you in just a tick.' Aisling reminded herself she'd come downstairs not just to get to the bottom of what was upsetting Mrs Flaherty but also to ensure their obnoxious guests didn't get bopped with the frying pan. Mind, that finger clicking had her tempted to give them both a clout with it herself.

Depositing the dishes on the worktop beside the sink, Aisling took a few of the calming yoga breaths Roisin had taught her and leaving Mrs Flaherty to her sizzling rashers, she left the sanctuary of the kitchen to take the rudest guests to have stayed at O'Mara's in a good while's breakfast order.

'We meet again,' she bared her teeth in what she hoped was more smile than grimace, hands clasped in front of her bottom clenched for no good reason other than she was uptight. 'Now I trust you've had time to peruse the menu?' For some reason, her voice had taken on plummy tones.

'You don't have many gluten-free options,' Sienna sniffed.

If you didn't add toast, wasn't everything on the menu gluten-free? Aisling wasn't sure, but she'd not let Arse and Arsier here frazzle her.

'I suppose I'll just have the fruit salad,' Sienna sniffed a second time. 'I hope it's fresh and not from a tin.'

'We all but picked it ourselves.' Aisling's face was beginning to ache.

'And, I'll have poached eggs served on a bed of asparagus.'

'I think you'll find that's not on the menu, sir.'

Ralph scanned the list as though expecting it to miraculously appear.

'But we can serve it on a bed of toast, and Mrs Flaherty fries a lovely tomato.'

'Fine,' he sniffed. 'I suppose that will have to do, and we'll share a pot of tea.'

'Loose leaf, English breakfast,' Sienna added, passing the menu back to Aisling, who took Ralph's from him, too.

As Aisling returned to the kitchen, muttering, she overheard, 'Please don't sulk, Ralph. What did you expect? It's not the Shelbourne. Of course, they wouldn't have asparagus.' It took all her strength not to fling back at them that Sienna should be fecking well grateful they'd no asparagus because it would only give Hooray Henry there the smelly wee. Aisling was a professional, however, and instead kept it buttoned and stomped through to the kitchen where Mrs Flaherty received the order as expected with a 'fecking fruit. What sort of a person eats fruit for breakfast?'

Aisling was glad she'd had the foresight to pull the door behind her as she set the kettle to boil and dug out a bag of loose-leaf tea. Then, she got to work on chopping and dicing the only apple, orange and slice of melon in the fridge, given most of their guests opted for a fry-up and not the token continental breakfast.

'This is for the two American brothers out there,' Mrs Flaherty said.

Aisling left her half-diced apple to carry their breakfasts, which were received with more courtesy than when the posh pipe cleaners had placed their orders.

When she returned, the cook was sawing into the black pudding like a lumberjack felling a tree. A grimace on her face.

Aisling frowned. 'Is everything alright, Mrs Flaherty?' She'd give herself the tennis elbow or a frozen shoulder the way she was carrying on.

'What are you on about Aisling? And what are you doing standing about gawping at me? That apple will have browned at the rate you're going.'

Aisling took the hint and carried on slicing and dicing the rest of the fruit. 'You just don't seem yourself is all.' How could she word this without causing offence? 'You seem, erm, well, you seem a little on edge.'

'I'm grand, so I am. Happy as a pig in muck, me.'

Aisling would have to take her word for it, so she tossed the orange and melon into the bowl.

Mrs Flaherty piled bacon onto a slab of thickly buttered bread, added a squirt of HP sauce and slapped another slice down. Then she passed it over to Aisling.

'Mm, this is gorgeous, thank you,' Aisling mumbled through her mouthful.

Dunking the frying pan in the sudsy water, Mrs Flaherty watched her out of the corner of her eye as Aisling leaned against the worktop, devouring it with satisfaction. People got older, but there was always a glimpse of the child they'd been in their faces, no matter their age. Looking at Aisling, she could now see that little girl who used to come down to the kitchen and hide in the dumbwaiter for a spot of peace and quiet, munching on a rasher sandwich, her nose in a book. Mrs Flaherty doubted she'd much time for reading these days with those bonny babbies of hers and turning her attention to the pan in the sink, she picked up the scrubbing brush with a grimace.

The breakfast rush was over, and she'd hang her pinny on the back door once she'd cleaned up and head home, but not before she'd given Aoife and Connor a cuddle. She was as fond of the new generation of the O'Mara family as she was of the last. Which was why she'd just fibbed to Aisling. Aisling was a worrier, always had been, and she'd enough on her plate with her little family without worrying about the guesthouse's breakfast cook on top of it all. She gritted her teeth and gave the pan what for despite the pain radiating through her hands.

The thing was, Mrs Flaherty wasn't fine at all.

Chapter Seven

♥

The tang of salt was on the tip of her tongue thanks to the stiff breeze coming straight off the harbour as Roisin, head down, hands thrust in the pockets of her Bendy Yoga Ladies jacket, hurried along. She'd drawn quite enough attention to herself for one morning, she thought only vaguely aware of lights twinkling invitingly inside the boutique shops, tinsel and sparkly baubles decorating their windows. Christmas seemed to come earlier each year. December was still ages away.

Now the school rush was over, the roads were quietish, and the pace of life noticeably slower than it had been in London. Roisin was happy to have stepped away from the treadmill of her old life because sometimes she'd felt like Mr Nibbles spinning around on his hamster wheel, never really getting anywhere.

At first, she'd found it strange attuning to her new environment, but she was slowly getting used to it and was the happiest she'd been in a good while making a new life here with Noah and Shay. Things would be close to perfect if not for a certain person's constant input.

Roisin had opted not to go back to Mammy and Donal's after the doggy debacle. She'd have only been waiting about for her to warm up under a hot shower and put on dry clothes. Instead, she'd said she was happy to carry on down to the studio on foot, and sure, why didn't Mammy and Donal take some time out for each other, given how busy they'd both been helping Roisin and Shay get sorted and settled? Backing this up with, 'Go and have a nice pub lunch somewhere. I'll be grand on my own for a bit, Mammy.'

This was a purely selfish suggestion on Roisin's part because she desperately wanted to spend some precious time alone in her studio. Mammy wouldn't hear of it, though, dismissing her with a flap of her hand, saying there'd be plenty of time for pub lunches and the likes once the studio was established.

Mulling this over, Roisin felt guilty for thinking disloyal thoughts about her mammy. It was the Catholic in her. It was only down to her input she was realising her dream. It was just that somewhere along the way, the lines had blurred, and it had become Mammy's dream, too, and Roisin didn't want to share.

'Shoo!' she flapped her hand at a seagull swooping a little too close for her liking; it probably thought she was a giant shrimp in her pink jacket.

The sight of Howth's Catholic Church reminded her that Mammy had told her to earmark December 8th for the annual lighting of the Christmas tree. Noah would love it, she'd said, and it would be an excellent opportunity for Roisin to network, saying they'd have to mull over merchandising ideas because, in business, you had to think outside of the square. Well, Mammy had excelled herself where the jackets were concerned.

Roisin had far too much on her mind for thinking outside the square, she thought, side-stepping a gentleman rugged up against the cold; like whether the pavement sign she'd commissioned for the studio would arrive on time for the grand opening. She saw the crevice-like opening to the blink, and you'd miss it lane down which

Carrick's the Cobbler's was located and wondered how anyone would even find her studio if it didn't.

The cobbles down the lane were slick beneath her feet, and the bell jangled as she pushed open the door of the old-world shoe shop, calling out, 'Good morning, Cathal!'

The little man, her landlord now and whom Mammy was convinced was, in fact, an elf given his resemblance to the character in the Wishing Chair books Aisling used to devour, looked up from where he was scribbling something in a book, an order presumably. 'Good morning, Roisin.'

Rosemary Farrell popped up alongside Cathal like a jack in the box, causing Roisin's hand to fly to her chest. Jaysus, but the woman was sprightly, she thought. It must be down to that hip replacement she had. Rosemary's face was flushed, and she'd the look of someone caught with her hand in the biscuit tin, but Roisin didn't like to ask what she'd been doing down there.

'C'mere to me now, Roisin, and tell me how Noah's after getting on this morning and close that door behind you. You're letting the cold in,' Rosemary panted.

Roisin stepped inside the shop, breathing in leather and polish as she closed the door reluctantly, not wanting to get caught up chatting. News of the dog fight outside the gates of Howth's primary school was bound to spread, however, and with that in mind, Roisin gave the couple an abbreviated version of the sorry tale.

'Ah, well, now don't fret. There's no such thing as bad publicity,' Rosemary said.

It was precisely the sort of remark Mammy would come out with, Roisin thought. No wonder the pair were friends in a round-about, extremely competitive way.

'Where is Maureen? You two are thick as thieves these days.'

'Mammy had to go home and change out of her wet things, you know, from the bucket of water tossed over her and the dogs.'

Rosemary nodded sagely while Cathal answered the phone that had begun ringing.

'And your jacket looks very smart, turn around so.'

Roisin obliged.

'The Bendy Yoga Ladies.' Rosemary read out slowly as if Roisin wasn't aware of what was stamped on the back of her jacket. 'I read that without my glasses, so it's nice and clear. Sure, that will spread the word about the town. Maureen's after having one made for me, too.'

Thanks a million, Mammy, Roisin thought.

'And I've been letting the girls I know who've had the knee, hip, or both replacements done about the special classes you'll be holding.'

Then again, maybe Rosemary had a point about the publicity thing, and it was good of her to help drum up business. Roisin said as much. In fact, this morning, she would be putting the final touches to the class timetable. Now she thought about it, she had been thinking outside the square with some of the classes she offered. There was to be the gentle flexibility session Rosemary was interested in with her hip, and classes specifically for new mams. Donal had put the idea in her head with a passing remark about holding men's classes. Mammy had devised the smart marketing idea of embossing towels and drink bottles for those fellas who signed up for the year, given they'd not be keen on the pink jackets. However, this was stereotyping on Mammy's part, and she should have known better after befriending Bobby-Jean or Bobby-Gene, depending on his/her mood in Santorini. Roisin hadn't mentioned her plans for a weekly session aimed at highly strung children focussing on breathwork. Noah was to be her poster boy.

They'd enough smart marketing plans without adding lunch boxes or pencil cases into the mix.

Cathal put the phone down. 'Before I forget, you've some mail, Roisin.' He pointed to a couple of envelopes on the counter. 'And there was a delivery for you earlier. I told the man to leave the box upstairs.'

Hopefully, it was her sign, Roisin thought. 'Thanks, Cathal, although those there are probably bills.'

'Part and parcel of being a business owner, Roisin,' Rosemary said crisply.

Now that was something Mammy would say, Roisin thought, making her way over to the counter. She scooped up the envelopes, and a quick glance at the return addresses revealed they were indeed bills. They could be dealt with later. Right now, she wanted to head up to her studio, check if the delivery was her pavement sign and take some time to savour the sanctuary she'd created while Mammy was otherwise engaged.

'Right, then I'll head on up.' She moved back toward the shop door.

'I don't know why you don't just use the internal access door, Roisin.' Rosemary pointed toward the door that almost blended into the wall behind the counter. It opened onto the stairwell that could be accessed through a separate door from the lane next to the shop.

There was a simple reason she refused to use it, not that she'd put a voice to it and risk offending her landlord's live-in lady-friend. The reason was that Roisin intended to start as she meant to carry on. She didn't want to encourage using the internal door because the shoe shop was separate from the yoga studio. Most of all, she didn't want Rosemary yoo-hooing up the stairs when she was in the middle of a class. She kept this to herself and replied, 'Ah, no, sure, you're grand,

Rosemary. I'll use the lane entrance. It feels more professional because we're separate businesses.'

'Well, don't let me stop you then. We can't have you feeling unprofessional now.'

Roisin ignored the serving of sarcasm this response was dished up with and made her escape.

Chapter Eight

♥

The laneway was quiet as Roisin exited the cobbler's with her hand already in her bag, feeling around for her keys. Her fingers closed over them, and locating the correct one, she slid it into the lock. Before she did the jiggle needed to turn it, though, she took a second to admire the signage telling clients that behind this door and up the stairs was where they'd find her yoga studio. The plain black lettering contrasted perfectly with the cheery red door, and with a sense of anticipation, Roisin twisted and twiddled the key until she heard it click. Then, giving the door a good shove, she reminded herself to mention to Donal that it needed oil in the hinges or whatever you did to prevent a door from sticking. He was the closest thing to a handyman they had in the family, she thought, using her backside to push it closed.

Roisin took the steps two at a time where, at the top of the landing, another door was locked. This one opened without fanfare, and she stepped inside, grateful for the central heating being on a timer and, wary of letting the chill from the drafty stairwell follow her in, closed the door behind her. Her hand patted around for the light switch, and flicking it on, she admired the serene studio space with satisfaction.

Initially, when Mammy had dragged her here to check out Cathal Carrick's former abode, her heart had sunk. Her first impression upon sticking her head through the door had been of an oppressive, dark, cluttered flat frozen around 1970. The smell suggested the cobbler bachelor was handy with a frying pan and nothing else. Old fat permeated the very walls. The updated heating system being the only concession to modern times. Cathal, it had transpired, had an aversion to the cold. Aware her mammy's eyes were on her, Roisin closed her own and told herself to use her imagination. Opening them, she envisaged the living room stripped of its ugly old wallpaper and given a fresh lick of paint, the curtains replaced with light sheer drapes and the lighting updated. It could work, she'd thought excitedly.

Now, her mouth curved as she spoke out loud to the empty studio, 'And it has worked.'

As per the lease, Cathal's old bedroom had been incorporated into the living room, making ample space for the studio. The bathroom and toilet were perfectly functional, while the kitchen was an added bonus because Roisin planned to utilise it as an area where her new mams, who opted to bring their babies to class, could feed and settle them.

Roisin rolled out her yoga mat onto the floorboards discovered when, with Cathal's permission, the motheaten Axminster carpet was pulled up. A sand and varnish had brought them up to an umber-hued treat. The mellow aroma of botanicals that lingered from the scent diffuser instilled a calming sense of clarity and focus, and Roisin inhaled deeply.

She'd gone with the flow for most of her adult life, earning herself the family nickname Easy Osi Rosi. Now, finally, she was stepping up and taking life by the horns, so to speak. It felt good. Her phone ringing jolted her from her deep thoughts, and she frowned as her sense of calmness left the building. It had better not be Mammy telling her she was on her way and her eta (estimated time of arrival) once she'd found a park. However, a glance at the mobile's screen revealed it was Aisling, and sitting cross-legged on her mat, Roisin answered.

'How're you, Ash?'

'Grand. I was ringing to see how Noah got on this morning?'

Roisin forgot about her plan to soak up the ambience with some alone time as she replied, 'Have you all morning then?'

'I've an hour and a half, to be precise. The twins are down for their pre-lunch sleep. Connor took forever to settle, but he's out for the count now. Bless him, and I've a cup of tea and a bag of snowballs open beside me. I've found a new hiding place for them, so Moira's got no show of finding my stash, and don't be asking me where I'm keeping them because the fewer people that know, the less she can put the screws on.' At last, Aisling stopped to draw breath. 'So, c'mon, tell me what's after going down in Howth this morning.'

Roisin heard rustling and pictured her sister holding up and admiring one of the coconut, chocolate marshmallow treats she'd a weakness for before stuffing it in her gob. Where to start? She thought, deciding to begin with the unexpected visit from Mammy first thing.

'Roisin,' Aisling interrupted, hearing Mammy let herself in again. 'Moira and I both told you giving her a key to your house was an eejit move of the highest order. I mean, what were you thinking?'

'I know. I should have listened. But I thought if I was stuck at the studio, Mammy could pick Noah up from school for me and bring him home instead of around to hers and Donals.'

'But did you not think she'd see having her own key as a license to come and go whenever the mood takes her? What if you and Shay were doing the wild thing christening the kitchen or the living room or the like, and Mammy walked in?'

'At least she'd never do it again,' Roisin muttered darkly. 'I hope you and Quinn weren't after doing that at O'Mara's when he moved in because it's the family apartment you two are living in, remember? And you're not being helpful, by the way.'

'Well, I'm not one to say I told you so.'

'Aisling, you just fecking well did.' Roisin decided there was no point bringing up Mammy also having a key to the yoga studio because she wasn't likely to get any sympathy there either.

There was more rustling, and then, as her sister presumably spoke through her mouthful, she mumbled, 'Okay, look, the clock is ticking. What happened after Mammy bowled in?'

'She gave me a present is what.'

'Well, I hope she's one for Moira and me; otherwise, that's playing favourites, so it is.'

Roisin did a little grin. 'Oh yes, she's one for you and Moira. Don't you worry about that.'

'What's she after giving you then?'

'A jacket and yours and Moira's are identical, so you won't feel left out.'

'Ah, Jaysus. Is this going to be like the Chinese silk prostitute-style dresses?' Aisling referenced their mammy's gifts for her girls upon her return from a mammy-daughter trip with Moira to exotic Vietnam that had seen them looking like your American prostitute woman from the tele programme, China Beach. 'Let me guess. The jacket's in this season's hottest colour.'

'Wintergreen!' They chimed simultaneously, then laughed.

'No. It's not green. It's a shiny pink colour.'

Aisling groaned. 'I hope it's more dusty than salmon because salmon pink clashes something terrible with my colouring. It's alright for you and Moira with your Andrea Corr eyes and hair.'

'It's more shiny bubble gum pink, and Mammy has one too.'

'That's who youse both take after. Although Moira's eyes are more hazel than brown, like yours and Mammy's, I'm the odd one out, so I am.'

Aisling was indeed the anomaly in the family, with strawberry-blonde hair, green eyes, freckles and skin that would redden and refuse to tan, unlike her mam and sisters, who turned mahogany in summer. She took after their dear departed Nanna Dee in looks but mercifully not temperament, the old bite that she'd been.

Before Aisling could launch into an 'it's not fair' spiel, Roisin jumped in with, 'So does Rosemary Farrell and pink's definitely not her colour.' She was enjoying herself now, picturing the horror on her sister's face.

'Mammy and Rosemary Farrell have one, you say?' Trepidation had crept into Aisling's tone.

'Uh-huh.'

'Why?'

'The smart marketing. That's why. Mammy's had The Bendy Yoga Ladies stencilled on the back of the jackets. And so, as you know, you'll be expected to wear yours every time you leave the guesthouse, as will Moira because Mammy's a vested financial interest in my new yoga business.'

There was silence and then a 'Feck.' Swiftly followed by, 'I can't speak for Moira, but I'm never leaving O'Mara's again.'

'We're to be like the Pink Ladies from the Grease movie, only we're the Bendy Yoga Ladies. Mammy thinks it's a clever play on words on her part. As you can imagine, she's very pleased with herself and was strutting about the place with her Rizzo neck tie this morning looking the part.'

'She was not.'

'She was, too.'

There was a moment's silence, and then Aisling spoke up. 'Every cloud has a silver lining, Rosi.'

'Actually, the lining's white.'

'Feck off, you know what I mean. And I suppose at least this time I'll be part of the gang.'

'I knew you'd bring that up.'

'The jackets are karma for not letting me join your gang.'

'I knew you'd say that too. Well you've had your payback Ash because she made me wear mine on the walk to school.'

'Did she have hers on too?'

'Yes, and we were responsible for a close call at the round-a-bout. It was mortifying.'

Aisling sniggered.

'It's not funny, Aisling.'

'If it was me after wearing the pink jacket with Mammy, you'd be falling about the place.'

She'd a good point, Roisin thought.

'But what about the marketing? Was it worth the mortification? Did you drum up any interest for the studio, get any new class bookings, that sort of thing?'

'Oh, we drummed up plenty of interest, but not for my yoga classes.'

Aisling must have picked up on the gloom in Roisin's voice because she hesitated before asking, 'Will I need more snowballs for this?'

'I'd recommend it, and could you toss me a couple while you're at it.'

'I would if I could and don't go anywhere. I'll be back in two ticks.'

Roisin uncrossed her legs and stretched them out in front of her, waiting, knowing that Aisling wouldn't share her snowballs with her even if she sat beside her on the sofa. She didn't have to wait long for her sister to come back on the line.

'Right. I'm back. Tell me what happened.'

'Noah put himself in charge of Pooh, which saw him make a new friend along the way to school.'

'That's good,' Aisling interjected.

'True, but Pooh bolted when we got near the school because he spied a cockapoo he fancied. He tried to have his way with her, but a black labrador, George was his name, got jealous and attacked him. Mammy threw herself into the fray along with George's owner, and they both wound up getting drenched when Noah's teacher threw a bucket of cold water over them and the dogs.'

Roisin listened intently, waiting for her sister to comment on the morning's awful events, but she didn't hear anything. 'Ash?'

There was a snort, a gasp and a wheeze, and Roisin realised she was laughing. 'Aisling, stop laughing!'

'I can't, and oh Jaysus, Rosi, it's not good. You know what my pelvic floors have been like since birthing twins.'

'Cross your legs.'

'I am!'

Roisin held the phone away from her ear, waiting for her sister to get a grip on herself, and at last, with the odd hiccup, she calmed down.

'Honestly, Ash, it was like some nightmarish scene from a nature documentary about the mating habits of neutered dogs.'

'And now the poodle is clambering on the cockapoo but wait! They're not alone. They've been spotted by a labrador,' Aisling intoned her best David Attenborough, which wasn't very good but did the trick and made Roisin laugh.

'I suppose it was funny when you think about it. I did meet another mammy called Becca, who seemed nice and said she was interested in checking out the studio, so it wasn't all bad.'

'Where are you now?'

'At the studio. I wanted some time here alone because Mammy had to go home and see to her wet gear.'

'I'm looking forward to the party this weekend.'

'You'll have to wear your pink, bendy yoga ladies jacket. You do know that.'

'I suppose.'

'Don't be telling Moira about them. Leave it as a surprise, like.'

The sisters sniggered, partners in crime.

'Oh, I almost forgot,' Aisling said. Bronagh put through an SOS call this morning because Mrs Flaherty was in a foul mood, and we've fussy guests staying, so I had to go downstairs to keep an eye on things.'

'Mr Fox set her off?'

'Yes, he'd paid a visit, but I got the feeling something else was going on with her.'

'Did you ask her if everything was alright?'

'Of course, and she told me everything was grand. I didn't believe her, but short of threatening her with the rolling pin, if she doesn't talk, there's not much I can do if she doesn't want to tell me what's on her mind.'

'She's coming this Saturday to the grand opening. At least, I think she is. I invited her at any rate.' Half of Dublin was because Mammy put a welcome drink on arrival and nibbles to be served on the leaflets. They'd been handed out around Howth and left on the front desk at O'Mara's. Quinn had also taken them to the restaurant in case anyone was interested in hoofing all the way to Howth for a spot of yoga. 'I suppose I could have a quiet word and see if I can get to the bottom of it.' Roisin loved Mrs Flaherty. They all did.

'There's no harm in trying.'

'Did she make you a rasher sambo.'

'Of course. I am breastfeeding two babies, you know.'

Roisin grinned to herself. Whether she was or wasn't, it wouldn't make any difference. Ash would have snaffled it down.

'I do know, and aside from Connor's teething, how are my niece and nephew today?'

'They're grand. They had a lovely time with Bronagh and Freya this morning while I was downstairs with Mrs Flaherty.'

'Ah, I bet they did.'

'I think Bronagh's after giving Connor one of her custard creams to suck on, even though I told her they're not on the solids yet.'

'Did you find crumbs on his stretch-n-go or something?'

'No, but Bronagh looked very guilty when I came and got the babies.'

'Roisin! It's only me.'

'Feck, Mammy's here. I'll have to go.'

'May the force be with you,' Aisling squeezed in before Roisin ended the call.

Chapter Nine

♥

Maureen had been inside the studio for under five minutes. In that time, she'd inspected the toilet and bathroom with Roisin trailing after her, asking her what she was doing. Opening the fridge and checking how much milk was left in the container, she replied vaguely, 'I'm checking to see everything is as it was left yesterday.'

'Why wouldn't it be? No one's been up here since then.'

"Ah, but that's the thing, Roisin. You don't know that.' Seemingly satisfied the milk hadn't been tampered with, Maureen put it back where she'd found it.

'Er, I do, Mammy. There's only me and you who've got a key.' And didn't she rue the day she'd had the spare one cut!

Maureen tapped the side of her head. 'God gave you this for a reason, Roisin. Use it and think. Who else has access up the stairs, like?'

'Well, Cathal and Rosemary, obviously, but they've their own facilities downstairs.

'Old habits die hard, Roisin.' Maureen took herself through to the studio. 'Perhaps their kettle's on the blink, and they've popped up here to make a sly cup of tea or to do their business.'

Christ, on a bike! The next thing she knew, Mammy would put trip wire across the front door entrance and mark the milk container. And, what sort of business was she on about exactly? Roisin's eyes flicked wildly about the studio. Sometimes, Mammy was more cryptic than a crossword puzzle. 'Do you mean business as in doing the accounts, that sort of thing?' She asked hopefully.

'No, and don't play stupid with me, Roisin. You know what sort of business I'm talking about. Rosemary's a sly old dog at times. You've got to watch her.'

'Mammy, surely you're not after suggesting she and Cathal come up here for a, a,' Roisin couldn't bring herself to say it.

'To use the toilet, precisely.'

Roisin's shoulders sagged with relief. 'Oh. You had me worried for a minute.'

'What did you think I meant?'

'Never mind.'

'You talk in riddles sometimes, Roisin.'

Give me strength, Roisin thought, knowing she would regret asking but needing the answer. 'And why wouldn't they just use their own toilet?'

Maureen shook her head and repeated Roisin's name slowly three times. It was very annoying, Roisin thought.

'Because the shop's toilet's outside. Sure, if Cathal planned on being sat on it for a while in this weather, his dangly bits would risk frostbite. And the cold makes Rosemary's hip ache.'

Roisin sent up a heavenward thank you when Mammy's phone rang, ending the ridiculous conversation. She watched as, fetching it, she held it at arm's length, stabbing a button before pressing it to her ear and shouting into the mouthpiece. 'Hello there, Maureen O'Mara speaking.' There was a tiny beat of silence followed by. 'Moira, would you slow down? I can't understand a word you're on about it.'

Roisin decided she'd leave Mammy to it, her eyes alighting on the oversized cardboard box inside the front door. It was the delivery Cathal had mentioned, and surprised by how light it was, she carried it through to the kitchen. She shut the door on Mammy and Moira's conversation. Whatever was going on, she'd find out soon enough.

There was a pair of scissors Roisin had to zip out and buy for the purpose of opening boxes in the worktop's second draw down and sliding the blade through the tape. She opened the box eagerly.

Yoga straps, she saw rifling through the polystyrene chips, wondering why on earth they needed all that packaging. There were twenty of them, and she'd just finished laying them out on the table, ready to tick the invoice off, when Mammy burst through the door.

'That girl pushes my buttons, so she does.' Her face was mottled red.

'We all push your buttons, Mammy.'

Maureen ignored the remark. 'And, you're not in my good books either.'

'What have I done?'

'Ruined the surprise is what.'

The pink bendy yoga ladies' jackets! Roisin realised Aisling must have got straight on the phone to Moira after speaking to her to tell her about them. 'I wanted to share the excitement of the new jackets, Mammy.'

Maureen's brown eyes narrowed, and Roisin knew her sarcasm radar was scanning what she'd just said. It didn't pick up on anything worth biting back on because she replied, 'Well, your sister's not excited. She said she wouldn't be seen dead in a pink Bendy Yoga

Ladies jacket. She was harping on about it ruining her cool, art student image.'

Fair play, Moira was a pain in the arse sometimes. She was brave, though, answering back and putting her foot down. Unlike herself and Aisling, who were apt to roll over and give up their self-respect. 'So she won't be needing her jacket then?' Roisin wondered who the lucky recipient of her sister's spare one would be.

'Oh no, she'll be wearing her jacket alright and wearing it with pride.'

Roisin cocked an eyebrow. 'How'd you swing that then?'

'Your sister knows what sides her bread's buttered on.'

There were no flies on Moira right enough. 'What did you say to her Mammy?'

Maureen puffed up, pleased with herself, 'I told her we're a family, and as such, we pull together, and she said just because we're family doesn't mean she has to make an arse of herself. To which I replied that she should think on because she made an arse of me more times than I've had hot dinners when she was a child.'

Roisin watched her Mammy rifle through the filo-fax of memories before pulling out and holding up her trump card.

'Like the time we were in Brown Thomas, and she wet her knickers with excitement telling Father Christmas about the Cabbage Patch doll she had her heart set on. She was after sitting on the poor man's knee at the time.'

Roisin sniggered, remembering the incident. It had the added bonus of getting her, Aisling and Patrick out of the annual photo with the man in the red suit that year. They were teenagers at the time and far too old for that sort of carry-on. Not even Mammy could sway Father Christmas to let the rest of her children hide the wet patch by gathering around for just a 'quick snap, like.'

'Or the time—'

'I get the picture, Mammy.'

'Then I reminded her who it was looked after the toddler Kiera for her and Tom every Wednesday even though the change from Monday when I used to have her meant dropping my watercolour painting class?'

The three sisters had secretly rejoiced that Moira's class schedule time change meant that they wouldn't be gifted with monstrosities of Howth Harbour to hang on their walls this Christmas.

'But that's bribery Mammy.'

'Smart marketing is what it is, Roisin.'

'And you love having the toddler Kiera.'

'I do, and Moira will love wearing her new jacket.'

That signalled the close of the conversation, and Roisin gathered up the belts. 'Right then, I better crack on with the timetabling, and I haven't even checked the answerphone for new bookings yet.'

'Before you start on all that, I want you to come with me to pay Ciara with a 'C' from my boutique down the road like a visit.'

'I don't have time for clothes shopping, Mammy.'

'It's not for the clothes shopping; it's for the merchandising.'

Roisin sensed she wouldn't like whatever it was that came next.

'The pink jackets were made through a contact of Ciara's, and I want her to have a word in yer woman's ear about a discounted bulk order. Exclusivity is smart marketing.' Maureen's eyes glazed over. 'Think about it, Rosi, in exchange for signing up for a year's membership to the Bendy Yoga studio, you get a free pink Bendy Yoga Ladies jacket. Only it's not just a jacket. It's bigger than that.'

'It's a fecking big monstrosity, is what it is,' Roisin muttered, but it fell on deaf ears.

'It's a chance to belong, to be part of a, a, what's the word I'm looking for?'

'Girl gang,' Roisin supplied.

'That's two words, and don't be using the word gang, Roisin. It puts me in mind of the Hells Angels and the like.' She crossed herself. 'Group is what I was after. Think smart marketing.'

If she heard that phrase again this morning, she'd not be responsible for her actions, Roisin thought as Mammy bustled her back into her pink bendy yoga ladies jacket and herded her out the door.

Chapter Ten

♥

The foot traffic was heavier now than when Roisin had made her way to the studio earlier, and she could feel eyes burning into her back as she and Mammy made their way down Main Street. She thought they were certainly getting plenty of attention, glancing over her shoulder and catching a touristy-looking couple doing a double take as they read the wording on the back of their jackets. Their pink colour was eye-catching, and the fact they were matching was garnering interest, to be sure. Thinking about it, Roisin couldn't deny the jackets were having more impact than handing out flyers. People balled those up and binned them when they thought you weren't looking. It pained her to admit it, but there was a strong chance Mammy was right. The jackets were smart marketing. Not that she'd be telling her that!

Pooh wasn't with them this time, which, after his performance outside school, was a blessing. He was worn out from his shenanigans earlier, Mammy said, and she'd left him curled up on his doggy bed with the country music compilation CD playing for company. He didn't like being alone, and Donal had ducked out to band practice.

Donal fronted The Gamblers, a Kenny Rogers tribute band, owing to his strong resemblance to the great man and his ability to hold a tune. They would be performing gratuitously at this weekend's grand yoga studio opening. Given they'd had a lull in bookings this year, the band wanted to brush up. Mammy, who played the tambourine and accompanied Donal on the Dolly Parton and Sheena Eastern duets, said she'd been practising her parts in the shower and that playing the tambourine was like riding a bike. It all came back to you once it was in your hand. Personally, Roisin would rather Shay's group, The Sullivans, were playing. However, she would never say this for fear of hurting Donal's feelings.

Roisin halted, feeling a tug on her sleeve. 'Were youse two the foreign mother-daughter duo in the Eurovision Song Quest last year?' An elderly lady peered out under her lilac felted wool hat at Roisin.

'Pardon?' Roisin didn't think she'd heard the question correctly. The woman's words had caught on the arctic wind gusting but had sounded like she'd asked something about Eurovision.

A keen pair of button blue eyes sized Roisin and Mammy up, and Roisin registered the little lady's coat was the exact shade as her hat and set off the pretty pink blush in her cheeks. She repeated her question slowly and loudly as Mammy did when encountering someone for whom English was not a first language. 'I asked if you were the mother-daughter duo in the Eurovision last year because you're the spit of them, so you are.' She gave them both the once over. 'Are youse off to do a matinee performance because you look the part in those jackets? If I were your manager, I'd suggest you wear the spandex trousers on stage. You know, the sprayed-on ones, not those baggy kneed yokes you've got on there.' She frowned, pointing to their respective Mo-Pants.

Maureen nearly tripped over her feet hearing this. She was a massive fan of Eurovision and could be found glued to the television

screen each year. As such, she wasn't offended by the reference to their
Mo-Pants being baggy-kneed.

'Only I thought you were Eastern European from one of those
countries beginning with 'S.' So, are you touring, like? Because I'd pay
money to see youse singing the song. Very catchy it was. I hope you've a
few more in your repertoire because you couldn't be singing the same
song over and over for a whole show, could you now? People would
get fed up.'

Roisin suspected the woman wasn't quite right. Still, she imme-
diately worried that she might put ideas in Mammy's head because
Mammy was easily influenced. Ah, Jaysus! The next thing she'd know,
Mammy would have her, Aisling and Moira performing for Ireland as
The O'Mara's instead of The Nolans at the next Eurovision. They'd be
two sisters short, meaning Mammy and Bronagh would have to step in
as the missing two unless Mammy flew Cindy in for the gig, in which
case Bronagh would be stood down. This needed to be nipped in the
bud right now, she thought, stepping in. 'No. We're not the mammy
and daughter duo from Eurovision, but we are Mammy and daughter.
It's a yoga studio we're after opening, well, I am.'

'We're business partners. I'm the silent partner,' Maureen butted
in.

Chance would be a fine thing, Roisin thought. 'The studio's called
The Bendy Yoga Studio. That's what the jackets are for.'

'And the spray-on spandex pants don't breathe very well. They'd be
no good for the yoga, like.'

'The studio opens next Monday,' Roisin added, wanting the final
word.

There was no such thing with Mammy, though she thought, eye-
balling her as she said, 'But we're having a grand opening party on

Saturday afternoon, and we'd love to see you there. The more, the merrier.'

'A party, you say?' That saw the little lilac lady stand to attention.

'A party,' Maureen confirmed.

Roisin watched a small plane flying overhead and thought Mammy might as well have a banner attached to it advertising the party to all and sundry. The costs for the thing escalated with each passing day because a dozen frozen supermarket savouries and a glass of fizz wouldn't cut the mustard.

'And will I get a complimentary jacket like yours if I come?'

Jaysus wept! Roisin thought they'd a shrewd one here.

'No. But if you purchase an annual studio membership entitling you to unlimited classes, you will.'

The lilac lady wasn't bothered about memberships and the like as she got straight to it, 'Will there be free drinks and food?'

'There will be plenty of nibbles and a free drink upon arrival.'

'Well, if you're sure to make sausage rolls and have a bowl of the little red sausages and sauce, I'm partial to those, then I'll come. I've a few friends who might be interested, too, although you'd want something sweet on offer but not creamy. At our age, the cream's too rich. It plays havoc with our poor old tummies.'

'Sausage rolls, little red sausages and something sweet but not creamy.' Maureen tapped the side of her head. 'It's all up here.' Then, she whipped out one of the studio business cards they had made up for this purpose and handed it to her. 'That's got the studio's address on it, and the party's kicking off at three o'clock sharp.'

'Grand. I'll see you then.' Miss Lilac 2002 trundled on her way.

'Mammy,' Roisin squared up to her hands on hips. 'What did you invite her and her friends for. She's not the sort of client we're trying to attract. Yer woman there's the sort who turns up at funerals for folks she doesn't know for the free food.'

'But she might have a yoga-type daughter, Roisin, and tell her all about the new studio. And besides, what's to stop you from running classes for seniors? I thought you weren't going to discriminate.'

'I already am. You and your lot are seniors, Mammy.'

'I meant senior, seniors, as you well know.'

'I suppose there's the chair yoga.'

'There you go!' Maureen was triumphant. 'You've got to think outside the square regarding the smart marketing, Roisin.' She drew a square in the air with her index finger.

'You're not Marcel Marceau, Mammy.' Roisin grumbled. It was a very annoying gesture on her part.

'I better check my phone to see if Pat's after ringing.' Maureen did so, squinting at the screen. 'No word. And we can't be standing about on the street gabbing when we've business to see to. Yer woman's chat about cream reminded me. We'll call at the café and pick up a cream slice for Ciara to sweeten the deal. She's partial to a cream slice.'

'So am I.' Roisin and her sisters were convinced Mammy was after spending a sizeable portion of their inheritance on cream slices for Ciara with a 'C' from her favourite Howth boutique. Not to mention covering her weekly wages due to her quest to keep up with the latest fashions.

'This isn't about you, Roisin, and yoga teachers wouldn't be after jamming cream slices in their gobs, now would they? You can choose something suitably seedy.'

'Thanks a million, and they wouldn't be jamming sausage rolls and little red sausages in their gobs either, but thanks to you and your wan in lilac back there, we'll be serving them up at the party now.'

'Don't be arguing with me, Roisin, or you'll get nothing.' Maureen strutted off.

'Mammy.' Roisin called after her. 'Why are you walking like one of the Bee Gees in the Saturday night fever video?'

There was no response, and Roisin hurried after her, following her inside the café. Its nautical theme always made her feel a little seasick, and she was relieved when they exited minutes later with a squidgy cream slice each for Maureen and Ciara and a flapjack for Roisin. No seeds were in it, but Mammy was satisfied the oats gave off the right vibe.

Once they'd reached the boutique Ciara oversaw, Maureen paused to admire the long-sleeved dress displayed in the window. 'It wouldn't be any good for me though. It's not the wrap style,' she said, opening the door. Ciara was flipping through a magazine at the counter when they stepped out of the cold. She looked up as they entered and spotted the paper bags Maureen was toting.

'Mo-mo, you shouldn't have,' she said, reaching for her share of the goodies.

Mo-mo? Roisin frowned. She'd be telling her sisters about this new nickname. It was only two vowels away from 'Ma-ma.' Jaysus wept. Mammy might even make her the fourth O'Mara sister in the Eurovision lineup!

Through a mouthful of cream, Ciara mumbled. 'I've a lovely new wrap-style top that just came in this morning. It's in this season's hottest colour, and I'm telling you, Mo-mo, you'd look gorgeous in it.'

Roisin ignored the pair as they chatted about the merits of the wrap style and tucked into her flapjack.

Mammy and Ciara had got their slices down in record time, and when Ciara ducked out the back to fetch the blouse she'd not had a chance to put on the rack yet, Roisin got a telling off.

'Don't be putting crumbs all over the floor.'

Ciara returned holding up the wintergreen blouse, and Maureen looked to Roisin, her eyes gleaming. 'It's very elegant so. I could wear it to the grand opening on Saturday, with my Mo-pants. What do you think Rosi?'

Grudgingly, Roisin had to admit her mammy would look well in it, but then she reminded her they hadn't come here to shop.

'Don't be talking with your mouth full, Roisin. I didn't raise a heathen. She's got a point, though, Ciara. It was a word in your ear I was wanting.'

Maureen explained her idea for bulk-buying the Bendy Yoga Ladies pink jackets.

'That's smart, Maureen.'

'Smart marketing is what it is, Ciara.'

Roisin mouthed the phrase along with Mammy and left them hashing the finer points out of Ciara's cut from the deal because it seemed a cream slice wouldn't do it. She checked her phone.

There was a text from Shay, and she hugged the phone to her chest after reading three simple words. It wasn't, 'I love you.' But it was every bit as sweet, and she re-read the message while holding the phone out again. 'I'll cook tonight.'

Shay's cooking wasn't a novelty. He enjoyed whipping up a meal and took charge of the kitchen regularly. What was a novelty was someone wanting to cook for her. The only time during her married life she'd had dinner made for her had been when she and Colin dined out, went to his mother's or when she came home to Ireland for a visit. To Roisin's mind, having a meal prepared for you, no matter how simple, was an act of consideration, something that hadn't featured in her marriage, and this meant more to her than any bunch of flowers or showy gesture. A warm glow settled over her because while Mammy might be driving her potty, now they were living near one another, she wouldn't change a thing.

As Maureen insisted Roisin try a wintergreen sweater to wear to Saturday night's party, she edited her previous thought because she might tweak things just a little!

Twenty minutes later, Roisin and Maureen left the boutique armed with shopping bags containing matching wintergreen tops and a verbal agreement for the manufacturing of the Bendy Yoga Ladies jackets. Maureen had also been commissioned to make Ciara a Christmas cake as her mammy wasn't much cop in the kitchen.

It had been a relief to hear that Mammy had cleared her calendar tomorrow to roll up her sleeves and get baking. A Mammy-free day! However, Roisin's face clouded when she heard her say she'd make three generous cakes. One for herself and Donal to share with Roisin and Shay, one for Moira, Tom, Aisling and Quinn, and one for Ciara and her fella. Ciara was officially being lumped in with the immediate family now. Aisling and Moira would be hearing about this! Roisin vowed, stepping outside the boutique with a scowl.

A woman with a child in tow crossed herself as they passed. Roisin hoped what Rosemary had said about no such thing as bad publicity was true, as she overheard the woman telling the child about the dangers of cults and how one of the signs to watch out for was matching clothes and the like.

Chapter Eleven

N oah was sitting at the kitchen table with his legs swinging underneath it, his face animated as he told Shay all about the dog fight at the school gates that morning.

'My new best friend Olwyn told me Pooh sexed the other dog, and then the black dog thought it was his turn, only Pooh wasn't having it.'

Shay's wine went down the wrong way.

'Noah!' Jaysus wept, Roisin thought. She wasn't ready to explain the facts of life to him just yet. Olwyn was obviously in the know, however.

'It's true, Mummy.'

In times like this, Roisin wished she had a Parenting 101 manual hardwired into her brain. For want of something to say, she muttered, 'I don't like your choice of words, Noah.'

Noah wasn't bothered, and he told Shay all about his new teacher, having given Roisin and his nan the run down when they'd met him after school. Roisin hadn't made eye contact with Dennis, the dentist, or Philomena of the Parents & Teachers Association.

'And we have a pet day in April, so I can take Mr Nibbles and Stef to see where I go to school.'

Ah, no! Roisin snapped to attention. School visits, where the gerbils were concerned, never went well. They were the Houdini of the gerbil world, and the last time Noah had insisted on taking Mr Nibbles to school, he'd escaped and been found hiding out in the toilets. He'd a thing about toilets. Still, she'd enough on her plate just now, and spring was months away. She realised in that way of children when they keep up a non-stop chatter that Noah had changed the subject and was telling Shay his new favourite dinner was 'ghetti boganase.' His red-rimmed, tomato-sauce lips were confirmation of this. Although, given his monologue, Roisin didn't know when he'd stopped talking long enough to put any food in his mouth.

'Just call it spag bog, Noah,' Shay grinned over his wine glass. 'And I'm pleased you're enjoying it.'

'Spag bog is my new favourite dinner, but only if you make it, Shay.' Noah lowered his voice to a whisper as if Roisin, sitting directly opposite him, couldn't hear as he added, 'Mummy's tastes like poos.'

'Thanks a million, Noah.' Roisin paused, mid-twirling ribbons of pasta around her fork, affronted. 'I'll remember that, son.'

'Good, because I think Shay should make the spag bog from now on, Mummy. You should write it on there.' A splatter of sauce landed on the table as he pointed his fork at the fridge door where the hand-written House Rules the three of them had nutted out together the day after they'd moved in were held in place by colourful magnets. Roisin thought Noah should have input about the day-to-day rubbing along harmoniously stuff. It was a way to make him feel his opinion mattered in his new family set-up. The list, however, was growing, and she was beginning to regret her bright idea.

'I'll write it up after we've eaten,' she said through gritted teeth.

Shay smirked as he forked up a mound of noodles, and she poked her tongue out at him.

Satisfied, Noah cleaned his plate, licking it when he'd finished.

It was overkill on his part, Roisin thought. She got the message.

'What's for pudding?' His bright eyes shone hopefully.

Roisin had never worried about pudding, but he'd been spending a lot of time with his nana, who thought pudding should be a staple after dinner. She'd helpfully informed her grandson that his mummy had enjoyed pudding each night throughout her childhood, and pudding had soon appeared on the House Rules. 'Erm,' she mentally foraged through the pantry and freezer, coming up with, 'ice cream and fruit.'

'Just the ice cream will be plenty, Mummy, thank you. Please may I be excused?'

'Nice try, Noah. It's fruit and ice cream or no ice cream, and yes, you may.'

The phone rang as he carefully carried his plate to the worktop, and she watched him proudly. He was learning.

'I'll get the phone!'

'It's probably for you anyway,' Roisin called, hearing him breathlessly answer, 'Hello, Noah Quealey speaking.' Then a nanosecond later, 'Granny! Mummy, it's Granny!'

'Say hello for me,' Roisin shouted, pulling a face. No love was lost between her and Colin's mother, but Noah's granny loved him, and Roisin would never come between them. So far as she was concerned, the more people in her son's life who loved him, the better. Besides, she felt sorry for the woman who, in the space of a few months, had lost her son to the Emirates and her grandson to Ireland. That didn't mean she wasn't dreading the inevitable visit!

It was only a matter of time before Elsa Quealey announced she was coming to see their new home in Howth. She was already making vague threats about booking her flights after Christmas once they'd had a chance to settle in properly. Awkward was the word that sprang to mind at the idea of her being here with Shay, not to mention Mammy, who'd never warmed to Elsa. Like Pet Day, she'd cross that bridge when she came to it. One day at a time, Roisin, she told herself. Shay distracted her from her thoughts by asking how her day had been.

She smiled at him. 'My day? Well, it was interesting. I've learned a thing or two about business and smart marketing.' Roisin pointed to her diminishing pasta and Bolognese sauce mound, 'And Noah's right. This is delicious.'

'My mam's secret recipe. And smart marketing. That sounds like something Maureen would say.'

Roisin grinned. 'It is. She's driving me mad saying it every five minutes, but then I saw the power of branding first-hand. So, even though I felt like a complete eejit parading about Howth in my Bendy Yoga Ladies pink jacket, I think it's a small price to pay for attracting clients to the studio.'

'I told you pink suited you,' Shay winked and shovelled in a mouthful of noodles.

God, he was sexy, even if he did have sauce on his chin. Roisin melted, wondering how he managed to look gorgeous chewing. She had him in bits, relaying the tale of the lady in lilac and the Eurovision Song Quest conversation, following it up with the story of the woman crossing herself on the main street and warning her child of the dangers of cults as she mistook herself and Mammy for members of a new sect. 'And how was your day?'

'Not as eventful as yours by the sound of it.'

'Borrow Mammy for a day. The eventfulness never stops, and I want to hear about your day, eventful or not.' She listened with her head tilted as he told her about the gig The Sullivans were booked for in Galway the weekend after next and how the festival arrangements were panning out for Green Fields in Laois next July. When he'd finished, she got up from the table in time to catch Noah telling Granny Quealey about Pooh sexing the little dog at the school gates and how his Nana had got a bucket of water poured over her when his new teacher threw it at the dogs. Roisin froze, counting backwards silently: three, two, one...

'Mummy! Granny wants to talk to you.' Noah stampeded back into the kitchen with the phone in hand.

Roisin glanced at Shay, seeing him mouth, 'Good luck.'

She'd need it. The evening had been lovely so far, and she'd no wish to spoil it by having words with Elsa. Steeling herself for a conversation with her ex-mother-in-law, she took the phone from her son's outstretched hand and ventured out to the hallway, sure to close the door behind her. She suspected Noah would take advantage of her being otherwise engaged and try his luck with the ice cream-only pudding scenario with Shay. Ah well, what she wasn't privy to, she wouldn't mind. Then, injecting warmth into her tone, she spoke up, 'Hello Elsa, how're you?'

'Much the same as I was the day before yesterday, Roisin.' Elsa Quealey wasn't a woman who wasted time on pleasantries, and the question wasn't reciprocated. 'What's this doggy business at the school gates Noah's on about? He's far too young to be spouting off about the facts of life. I don't mind telling you I was shocked hearing him use that language. I didn't discuss the subject with Colin until he was fifteen.'

Roisin resisted the temptation to reply, 'That's because he was still playing with his Lego until he was fifteen.' And she knew there'd been no conversation. He'd been handed the Where Do I Come From? book. Elsa had probably only given him that because she'd caught him doing something inappropriate with his Princess Leia and Luke

Skywalker figurines, she thought nastily. Her ex-mother-in-law didn't bring out her best qualities. 'He was after telling you about an unfortunate incident outside school this morning and relaying what his new friend said to him. You know what a parrot he can be.' She heard a sharp intake of breath at the other end.

'What sort of a school are you sending him to, Roisin?'

In the past, her mother-in-law had walked all over her with her bullying ways, but that was the past. The tables had turned with Colin leaving, and Roisin wouldn't allow herself to be pushed around. 'It's a perfectly grand little school.'

'So you say. I'll see for myself soon enough.'

Roisin forgot to breathe, only inhaling when Elsa added, 'But in the meantime, I suggest you thoroughly vet any potential new friends of Noah's. You can tell a lot about people from the cleanliness of their home.'

Was that a dig because being house-proud wasn't one of Roisin's shining qualities? Her toes curled inside her slippers. The woman was such a snob!

'The ties children form at this age are important. You don't want Noah running with a fast crowd.'

This time, she choked back a snort of laughter. 'Noah's six, Elsa. I don't think we've any worries there, but I'll be sure to get to know the parents of his new friends. Don't you be worrying your head, like. Now I'll have to love you and leave you.'

'Before you go, I wanted to talk to you about Christmas.'

Roisin's toes began cramping. 'I've not had a moment to think about it, to be honest, Elsa, what with the studio opening.' Colin was making noises about coming home to stay with his mother for Christmas, and they wanted Noah to join them. Roisin was reluctant because this would be his first Christmas here in his new home. She was hoping for a compromise. Perhaps he could go to London for boxing day and have two Christmases. But for now, she was stalling until the party on Saturday was out of the way.

'Roisin time is ticking. Plans will have to be put in place.'

'Listen, Elsa, it's been lovely talking to you,' Roisin lied through her teeth, 'but I've got to get Noah upstairs and in the bath. He's had a big day and needs to be in bed on time.'

'Quite right.'

Finally, something they could agree upon. 'Right, so I'll pop him back on to say goodnight to you, shall I?'

'Christmas?'

'I'll get back to you next week.'

No reply was forthcoming, so Roisin carried the phone to the kitchen, where her son was scraping the remnants of ice cream from a bowl. 'Bye then.' Holding her hand over the receiver, she told Noah his granny wanted to say goodnight to him. Noah took it from her.

'Granny, you haven't said hello to Mr Nibbles and Stef yet.'

She watched him hurtle out the door, hearing his footsteps racing up the stairs. Then, turning back to Shay, she saw he was getting up from the table, his pullover sleeves pushed up in readiness for the dishes.

'Shay.'

'Mm,'

'I'll wash up.' Three little words, Roisin thought. That was all it took to show someone you cared.

'Thanks. I've a call to make, and then what do you say we make it an early night?'

'I think that sounds grand.'

She carried her plate over to the sink and, turning around, said three more little words. 'I love you.'

'Love you too.'

Chapter Twelve

T he road was quiet by Dublin standards at this time of the
morning, the footpath deserted and parking a breeze. In fact,
there weren't many mornings Mrs Flaherty couldn't pull up in
the white Fiesta she'd owned since the early eighties right outside
O'Mara's. On those rare occasions her spot was taken, she never
wound up nosing her trusty little car in alongside the kerb more than
three doors down.

The Fiesta had seen better days, but it never let her down and still
got her from A to B, or rather from home to the guesthouse without
bother. So when the mister made noises about upgrading it, she closed
her ears. Besides the dent in the front fender where a gatepost suddenly
appeared, and the mysterious ding in the back bumper ensured nobody ever boxed her in. So, yes, the car, dings and dents and all, suited
her fine.

What didn't suit her fine, though, was the deep ache radiating
through her hands. Pulling the safety belt across this morning had
been a struggle, and just holding the steering wheel had been a trial.
Tears of frustration had threatened, and expletives were murmured
before she turned the key in the ignition. Just for a moment, only a

moment, she'd been tempted to go back inside her darkened house where John Joseph was still snoring, admitting defeat.

Polly Flaherty had been christened Mary, but Polly she'd always been, and she'd never been a person who gave in easily either. Her dear, late departed mammy would give an exasperated nod to that. Polly was always truthful, though she'd have said, but lately, Polly hadn't been honest with those who cared about her. Take Aisling enquiring as to how she was doing the other day. Her reply of 'grand' was a fib. The arthritis that plagued her joints had spread to her hands. And was steadily worsening. However, if she'd relayed this to Aisling, she would have told her she needed to make an appointment to see her doctor. Polly didn't like to bother him with her silly ailments, though. Doctor Barry was a busy man who had more important things to deal with than her moaning and groaning about old age and its many afflictions.

Then there was John Joseph. God love his soul. He meant well with hints about it being high time she hung up her pinny and gave her poor, work-worn hands a well-deserved rest. Sure, he'd say, she was a woman in her seventies, past retirement age. 'You've no need to be working, Pol.' He didn't understand that Polly liked to feel useful and that she was needed at O'Mara's. She was also part of the family, having been privy to the O'Mara girls' daily lives since they were small. They were an extension of her own family, with the only difference being her children were too busy getting on with their lives to find time for their old mam.

For the most part, she and John Joseph rubbed along happily enough, but they'd had words the other afternoon on this very subject. It had started when John Joseph had finished massaging the anti-in-flammatory gel into her sore hands. He'd sat back in his chair and suggested she tag along to the bowls with him to see how she liked it. 'You're frightened you won't know what to do with yourself if you hand in your notice at O'Mara's, Pol. Any fool can see that. What you need is a hobby. Sure, that's what being retired is all about. Having the time to do the things you enjoy, but with our brood, you never got a chance to find out what they might be.'

Now, Polly loved her husband of fifty years dearly, but he could be an awful thick eejit at times, and she took umbrage with being told what she should do. On top of that, wasn't he just after doing the lid up on the gel tube there, having seen her knobbly, swollen knuckles for himself? And there he was, looking all pleased with himself over his bright idea of her taking the bowls up with him. Polly had pointed out sharply that even if her fingers could fit in the holes of a bowling ball, she was far too competitive to trust herself in command of one. The bowls were his thing, not hers, and they weren't the sort of couple who liked to be joined at the hip. John Joseph had conceded her point with a nod of his head, which, when she thought about it, closely resembled that of a bowling bowl. If he'd left it at that, she wouldn't have shouted, but he didn't. Instead, John Joseph suggested perhaps she might be better suited to a craft of some description.

That was when she'd seen red thundering back at him with a sweet and merciful Jesus. Had he not listened to a word she'd said? Wasn't the whole point of the conversation they were after having her arthritis-riddled fingers? It was John Joseph, agreed meekly. So how was she supposed to hold the special needle for the felting work or scissors for the card making and the like? He'd taken himself off to the bowls early after that, and Polly had made the coddle for his dinner. John Joseph didn't like the dish, claiming it was a fancy name for leftovers.

With the memory of that conversation still fresh, Polly gritted her teeth and locked her car. A little arthritis in her fingers would not stop her from arriving here at the guesthouse where she'd worked since her children had grown up and flown the coop, arriving at the dot of six-thirty Monday morning through to Friday. Sure, there were people with far worse things to contend with than a spot of bother with their hands, and you'd not catch her complaining.

You could be forgiven for thinking it was still the middle of the night, Polly thought, making her way toward the front door, the keys in her hand. The street lights were on, and the sun wouldn't rise until closer to eight o'clock. If it decided to grace them with its presence today, that was. Given the smattering of drizzle on the windscreen as she made the short drive from the home where she'd spent all her married life in Phibsborough on the North side to the guesthouse, she wasn't betting on it putting in an appearance.

The dimmer light was on as she let herself into the reception area, and the warmth inside was like being greeted with a hug. She made sure to lock the door behind her, no sooner doing so than her nose began tingling from the heady scent of the lilies in the vase on top of the front desk. She didn't linger, reaching the top of the stairs leading to the basement before her sneeze exploded. It sounded loud in the silence, given the only other noise was the faint grumbling of the water pipes. Upstairs wasn't her domain. The kitchen was where she felt at home, so she made her way brusquely down the stairs.

Polly usually enjoyed her morning routine. She liked the peace of the half-hour between hanging her coat up and hearing the first foot-fall on the stairs, which signalled an early-rising guest with a business meeting or tour to be heading off on. It was a time for laying out the equipment and ingredients needed to whip up a breakfast that would line their guests' stomachs. She liked nothing more than to clear away their empty plates, knowing she'd set them up for whatever their day would bring. It was a routine she could have gone about blindfolded.

This morning, however, Polly first ran her hands under the hot tap to ease their stiffness. The relief was temporary, she knew, but it was enough to get her started.

Her habit was to make a brew for herself first thing, but the hot water boiler hadn't had a chance to begin whistling when her equilibrium was broken. Polly froze, egg carton in hand, as a clattering sounded in the courtyard outside the kitchen.

That fecking fox! Her eyes widened, and her blood began boiling. She set the eggs down and armed herself with the rolling pin despite the discomfit it caused her to do so. If the creature went for her with its sharp little teeth, she wouldn't be afraid to use it. With that thought in mind, she opened the door to the courtyard, heedless of the chill, as she poked her head outside. There, illuminated by the sensor light, was the bane of her life. The fox.

The animal's unblinking eyes fixed on hers. This was not their first encounter, and forgetting herself for a moment, Polly almost cried out as her grasp automatically tightened on the rolling pin, then slackened at the corresponding stab of pain. As for the fox, he was like a ginger statue alongside the rubbish bin. It was slim pickings this morning, and Polly wouldn't have thought that tiny sliver of bacon rind on the ground beside him was worth the danger run he'd undertaken for it. As the standoff continued, her breath was like a plume of dragon smoke on the frigid air. Who would give in first? She wondered, aware of sleeping guests and therefore not telling the creature in no uncertain terms to feck off back where it had come from.

The fox was the first to spring to life, and the sudden movement saw Polly jump and mutter under her breath. She watched his bushy tail trail on the pavers through narrowed eyes as he attempted to slink toward his point of entry and exit. He was petrified, she realised, as his eyes never left hers; not only that, but he was limping. It was this that had slowed him down. Unexpectedly, she felt a jolt of sympathy for the animal who was in pain, and the rigidness with which she'd been holding herself softened.

Instead of 'G'won with you,' she whispered, 'Are you hurt, like?' The sound of her voice immobilised the fox once more. Perhaps it was the uncharacteristic softness in her tone that did it. Droplets of drizzle danced in the beam from the sensor light in the split second before it flicked off. The darkness under which the little red fox had sneaked in had deserted him now to be replaced with a pixelated, gloaming. It was a blessing nobody was up and about because they'd think she'd lost the plot enquiring after a fox's health like so, Polly thought.

Polly Flaherty was many things, foul-mouthed for one. A habit inherited from a navvy father who'd worked on the building sites. He'd ruled the roost at home to the point of making her poor mam tremble with his bellowing. It was alright for him to shout and carry on, but if any of his girls had used the language he threw about, they'd have been given a slap. Polly wasn't one for analysing things but didn't have to think too deeply to know that her use of the odd expletive was a show of defiance. Once married and out from under her da's thumb, if she wanted to swear, she fecking well would. So yes, while Polly was many things, a cruel woman wasn't one of them. She didn't like seeing any of God's creatures suffering, not even the fox here.

There was little she could do for him, though, other than fetch him the leftover sausage she'd put on a plate in the fridge yesterday. She'd intended to take it home to John Joseph as a peace offering only she'd forgotten. She expected the fox to have disappeared when she returned with the fat pork sausage as he indeed had. Nevertheless, she tossed it close to the hole beneath the brick wall that led through to the Iveagh Gardens, where he made his home. She was about to return to the kitchen's warmth when a scuffling alerted her. He was back.

It was the twitching, pointed black nose she spotted first. Polly thought the poor thing was hungry, watching from the doorway as his head emerged through the hole. His glassy eyes met Polly's once more, whiskers quivering.

'C'mon now, fella, I know we've not always seen eye to eye, you and me, but you can have the sausage. I won't hurt you, I give you my word.'

Hunger won out, and the little red fox chose to believe the cook who had chased him off many times, wielding her rolling pin and uttering a string of expletives. He pulled himself back through the hole and limped toward the sausage.

The trust he was showing was oddly touching, and Polly leaned against the door frame, watching as he began snaffling the sausage. He must be getting on in years himself, she thought, because they'd history the pair of them. Was it age-catching up on him like it was her? It only seemed five minutes ago she was a young girl with her whole life stretching out before her. Her mind flitted back over the years, only settling when it landed on the night she'd met John Joseph. She'd danced until her feet had ached that night.

If the fox was surprised when she began to speak earnestly, he gave no sign as he polished off his breakfast. Polly knew, though, that if anyone overheard her one-sided conversation, they'd think her properly mad.

Chapter Thirteen

Dublin, 1953

Polly's back ached from a day's scrubbing and dubbing, fetching and carrying, not to mention preparing the evening meal at the McEntee's three-story Monkstown home where she'd been employed since she'd left school at fifteen. Oh, but she'd had a spring in her step the day she'd burst through the front door eager to tell Mam all about her new job. She wanted to soften that frown between her brows. It had deepened since Bridie moved out and no longer contributed to the coffers.

That was six years ago now, and while she enjoyed her work well enough, it was always a relief to clamber on board the bus and head home on a Friday afternoon. Polly fancied it was a good omen for the night ahead if she managed to find a seat. It boded well indeed if she got away with pinching her younger sister Deirdre's sparkly blue cardigan before leaving for the dance! It served Dierdre and her haughty ways right. Just because she worked in the fashion department of Clery's didn't make her any better than the rest of them.

As the bus rumbled past the familiar sights of her city, Polly patted the pocket of the smart greyish-blue uniform dress Mrs McEntee had supplied her with when she'd first started work at the house near posh Eaton Square. It was one of two, alternated weekly, ensuring her uniform was clean and starched each weekend, ready for Monday morning. Mam had let the hems down after she suddenly grew two inches at sixteen. Then, the waist had to be altered when she finally developed a few womanly curves at eighteen. 'You're a late bloomer, so you are Polly,' she'd said, head bent over her task.

The reassuring lump of her wage packet presented without fail to her mam as soon as she got in the door each Friday afternoon was still there. Her spends would be counted out and handed to her, while the remainder of her earnings were tucked away in the housekeeping tin. The location of which changed regularly to ensure da didn't get his hands on it.

Polly's eyes were trained outside the window she was sitting beside. This afternoon, she'd nabbed a seat. Now, if she could only tuck Deirdre's cardigan under her arm and get out the front door without her noticing, then tonight might be the night she finally met a fella worth dancing with. Time was running out for Polly because at the ripe old age of twenty-one, with no young man calling for her, she was at risk of being left on the shelf. Or, so Mam said. Polly explained that the pickings at the Friday night dances were slim, to which Mam had replied she should stop being so fussy. Polly fancied she'd just stopped short of trotting out that beggars couldn't be choosers.

'Charming,' she mouthed silently at her reflection in the bus window.

'Sure, Emer's husband Padraig's no oil painting,' her mam had gone on to say. 'But hasn't your sister a good a life over there in Drumcondra?'

Polly didn't want to settle, though. She wanted to fall in love. In her opinion, that wasn't too much to ask for, but it was one she didn't share with her mam.

It wasn't a rich Prince Charming she was after either, just a decent fella with a good heart that made hers flutter. Wealth didn't impress Polly, not anymore. She'd grown to understand that money made for an easier life and brought nice things, but that didn't necessarily make a person happier. Mrs McEntee was proof of that. However, that wasn't the case the day she'd raised the shiny brass lion's head to knock on the door of her house when she'd arrived hot and bothered for the interview. She'd been in awe of number 23 when she'd finally found it.

Polly had walked up and down the street, glad of the shade the tall trees lining either side offered on a day proving to be a summer scorcher. The slip of paper the agency had given her clutched tightly in her clammy hand as she searched for the address written on it. In the end, a cat found the house for her when it suddenly sprang from a hedge on her second sweep of the street. When she'd paused, unable to resist petting it or asking it whether it happened to know where number 23 might be hiding, she'd caught a glimpse of white behind the hedge and realised that this must be it.

Polly rapped on the front door twice, well, three times if you counted letting go of the lion's head and letting it fall back. Then, she'd stepped back to squint up at the three-storied building, thinking you could fit three of her family's Grangegorman terrace inside it. Mrs McEntee opened the door, a well-groomed woman around her mam's age but without the grooves of hard graft and worry between her eyebrows. As Polly was swept inside, she'd tried not to gawp at her surroundings because Mam always said her face was an open book, and she didn't want to appear gormless.

The interview had taken place in the front room overlooking the rose garden. It was the grandest room Polly had ever been in, and her stomach had churned anxiously from her perched pew opposite Mrs McEntee as she answered her questions. She'd listened as her potential employer had told her it was just herself and Mr McEntee at home these days. Her two children were both married. Polly had tried to stay focused, but her mind had wandered the way it was apt to do as she imagined what it would be like to grow up in a house this size with only one sibling. She fancied it would be lonely even if there were times when Deirdre was being particularly superior or when Mairead had still been at home and was bossing her, that Polly longed for a bedroom of her own.

Despite her nerves that afternoon, she must have come across as perfectly capable of the housework and preparing an evening meal for two each day, reassuring her potential employer that she wasn't afraid of hard work.

'We don't have a lot, you see, Mrs McEntee,' she'd said, hands clasped on her lap as she leaned forward earnestly. 'But my mam's a house-proud woman and a good cook. She's passed everything she knows on to me.'

Mrs McEntee's carefully made-up face didn't give away much. When the interview was finished, there was an awkward beat of silence. Then she'd asked crisply whether Polly could start the next day because their last girl had left them in the lurch without notice. Polly had nodded so hard she was in danger of giving herself whiplash.

How terrified she had been of accidentally knocking one of Mrs McEntee's porcelain figurines or banging the hoover into the grooves of the antique furniture legs. She'd soon grown used to her daily surroundings, though, and had concluded that having all these rooms to rattle around seemed a little pointless. The house and the things inside it were beautiful, but there was no life within its four walls. No love or laughter. Not even harsh, shouted words. It had the hush of a home where a wake was being held. Still, it wasn't her place to judge, and Polly was happy enough working for the couple.

Mr McEntee, a well-to-do Barrister, would tip his hat to her on his way out the door to his inner-city chambers in the mornings and wouldn't be home by the time she left. As for Mrs McEntee, she only saw her fleetingly coming and going from her never-ending round of ladies' lunches. Polly thought she must order lettuce leaves because there wasn't a pick of extra flesh on her.

The house being echoingly empty didn't bother Polly. She took it as a sign she was trusted and suspected that if Mrs McEntee was about to hear her singing over the top of the hoover or when peeling the potatoes, she might have been politely asked to quieten down!

The fact of the matter was Polly knew the McEntees no better now at twenty-one than the day she'd come for her interview. They may be aloof, but they were never rude to her, and they paid her without fail. She thought she'd no cause for complaint, her breath creating a misty patch on the bus's window.

Polly was so lost inside her head that she almost missed her stop, and she skipped off the bus, calling a thank you to the conductor before hurrying past the grim buildings of St Brendan's. The mental hospital lay behind a solid wall and locked gates. It was a rite of passage for the older siblings of the local children to terrorise them with the stories of the ghosts that roamed its corridors. Even now, Polly half expected a wispy apparition to reach through the gate's iron palings toward her, its face contorted in misery. 'Thanks a million, Mairead,' she muttered once safely passed. It was alright for her with her spooky stories. She lived miles away these days.

The first thing that hit Polly as she opened the front door of their little brick house and called out a hello was the salty reek of boiling bacon. 'Oi Mam,' she said cheekily, popping her head around the kitchen door where she knew she'd find her standing over the joint simmering in a pot on the stove. 'Could you not make a stew of a Friday? Is it any wonder I've not met Mr Right when I head out the door to the dance smelling like cabbage and bacon each week?'

'You've not met Mr Right, my girl, because you turn your nose up at any poor lad who looks at you.' She held her hand out for Polly's wage packet.

'It's not my fault they're all either stick insects or spotty with greasy hair.'

'Oh, so is it Montgomery Clift himself you're expecting to sweep you off your feet at the Hibernian Hall?' Money was doled back into Polly's upturned palm.

The two women bantered back and forth like so until the front door went, signalling her younger brother Jimmy was home. He'd not long started work on a construction site and, thus far, was making it home with his wages of a Friday night. Polly knew their mam was determined he would be rewarded with a hot meal on the table as soon as he'd had a wash. As for their da, well, when he'd grace them with his presence was anyone's guess. It always soured Polly's night if she let herself in the door with only seconds to spare until curfew to find him home. He'd be eating the dinner left warming for him, hoping to soak up the ale and avoid a banging head in the morning. No matter how quiet she tried to be, he always heard her calling her into the kitchen to lament how Juliette having entered the church was a waste, given she was the prettiest of his daughters. 'It should have been you, Polly, because you're not after getting any other offers,' he'd say, jabbing his fork at her.

Polly shook thoughts of her father away, dodging Jimmy's play-punch as she pushed past him in the cramped hallway, wanting to lay out her dress and raid Deirdre's side of the wardrobe before her sister arrived home.

Several hours later, as she waited beneath the lamppost near the Parnell Monument, Polly was in good spirits. It was where she always met her friend, Nuala. Several admiring glances had come her way already, and Polly was putting it down to the sparkly blue cardigan. She raised her hand to her mouth and puffed into it before sniffing it in the hope the peppermint had done the trick. Then, waving out as she spied Nuala, she forgot about her dinner of boiled bacon and the like. The two girls linked arms and caught up on each other's week as they made their way down the northern end of O'Connell Street to Parnell Square, where the A.O.H Hall was located.

A line was already snaking out at the front entrance when they arrived, and they tagged onto the end of the queue. Nuala was engaged, but her fella was working abroad until Christmas, and rather than sit in on a Friday, she enjoyed accompanying Polly to the dances. What she'd do if not for Nuala, Polly didn't know because all her other pals were married with babies on the way.

She wouldn't worry about threatening spinsterhood tonight, though, she decided as the line inched toward the innocuous door, which gave no clue as to the splendid ballroom within because tonight, anything could happen! That was the magic of the Friday night dances. Excitement jittered through Polly's veins as they finally got their tickets clipped and stepped inside the brightly lit grand old hall.

Maurice Mulcahy's Big Band was playing, and although they'd yet to begin their first set, the hall was packed shoulder to shoulder and hot. There was an air of expectancy. Polly and Nuala beamed at one another, eager for the dancing to get underway. Dancing was as good for the soul as attending mass!

The moment Polly first saw John Joseph Flaherty cutting a path toward her, the noise of her surroundings faded away. Later, she'd learn he worked on the docks. Even though he was a little rough around the edges that night, he might as well have been Montgomery Clift because as they foxtrotted and waltzed cheek to cheek, Polly knew she'd found her dreamboat.

Present

'Of course, I married him, and we've a good life, although a little more foxtrotting and waltzing in it would be nice. But I'm not complaining, you understand.' The raucous big band music faded, and Polly was misty-eyed with nostalgia. 'I just never expected to feel like this, you know. Old and headed for the scrapheap.'

The little red fox, the sausage long gone, was still there, listening, and Polly felt he would have given her a nod of understanding if he could. Then, with a flick of his tail, he was gone again, and she was left feeling like she'd dreamt the whole exchange. It was only when she stepped inside the kitchen, draughty now and closed the door, seeing the empty saucer on which the sausage meant for John Joseph had been, that she knew she hadn't.

Chapter Fourteen

'No pink jacket this morning?' An amused voice asked.

Roisin spun around, her hand still raised as she waved Noah through the school gates. This was his fourth morning at his new school, and he was swaggering like he owned the place. All her worries about him not settling in, given how much he'd loved his school in London, had been unfounded. As had her fears Colin's move to Dubai would leave him struggling with rejection issues. He spoke to his dad every Sunday and Wednesday night and would see him over the upcoming holidays. Something would have to be worked out. Noah was fine. Better than fine. Kids really were resilient, she thought as a wide smile spread across her face, seeing the blonde woman smiling at her. 'Becca, hi.' She'd hoped to run into her again, sensing a kindred spirit when they'd met briefly on Monday morning. 'And, no, I refuse to wear it unless I'm with my mam, then I've no choice. She calls the jackets smart marketing.'

'I remember her saying.' Becca looked pleased Roisin had remembered her name, and then she laughed. 'And, I think your mam and my mam are after having loads in common. Including pearls of wisdom for most occasions.'

'Or too much to say for themselves, depending on how you want to look at it.'

Both women laughed.

'You won't be seeing my mam in the mornings here though because I banned her from walking to school with myself and Noah after the dog fight on Monday,' Roisin supplied. She'd also hoped to run into Philomena of the Parent Association to smooth over any ill feelings but hadn't seen her since Monday morning either. Speak of the devil. There she was now, herding her numerous offspring out the back of a Land Rover. Nancy, the cockapoo's face was pressed to the passenger seat window, tongue lolling. Once her children, neatly turned out like little Von Trapp's, had kissed their mam goodbye, Philomena scanned the area, presumably for hormonally challenged poodles, before unloading her. She set the well-groomed dog down on the ground by her feet.

'You almost expect them to start singing about the hills being alive, right?'

Roisin laughed, watching the last of Philomena's children skip in the gates. 'You read my mind.'

'Believe it or not, they do sing. They're all in the church choir, the pony riding club, the gymnastics squad, the tennis club and the water polo team, as well as doing after-school French lessons and—'

'Stop! Jaysus.' Roisin shook her head. 'And there was me wondering whether Noah joining the local Cub Scouts and doing swimming lessons would be too much for him. Or more to the point, me, and how I would juggle them with the studio.'

Becca flicked her a smile of understanding. 'I hear you. I've always got two balls in the air and one rolling around on the ground.'

Roisin realised she didn't know anything about Becca's family other than her mam lived here in Howth, too. 'So you know Noah, who's six by the way, and I moved here from London, and I'm opening a yoga studio. Oh, and my mam fancies herself as the Howth businesswoman of the year. But what about you? Who've you got at the school here?'

'Just Lottie. She's Noah's age. I've only one, which right now is more than enough. Like I said, I always feel like I'm dropping a ball somewhere. I'm a medical receptionist in Sutton. It's part-time, but even still, it's hard to make everything work. I'd be lost without my mam on hand to help out.'

That explained the tailored blouse and skirt she wore today beneath the camel coat she'd admired the other day. Roisin only realised she'd unconsciously glanced at Becca's hand as she waggled her fingers. The tell-tale white band where a wedding ring had presumably been was conspicuous. She was embarrassed at being caught out. 'Sorry, I didn't mean to—' 'Don't be silly. Sure, you're grand. I'm in the process of getting divorced. Lottie's dad lives in Rathmines, in what was our family home.'

There was no mistaking the bitterness that had crept into her voice, and Roisin felt a stab of solidarity having been there and done that. She'd also long since packed up the ill-will she'd initially felt toward Colin. It wasn't good to hold on to old hurts. 'So am I. Divorced, that is. Noah's dad left London recently for work in Dubai. That's what brought us home to Ireland. We've set up home with my partner Shay who was living in Dublin. We got sick of having to always say goodbye to each other. Howth seemed like a fresh start for us both, and of course, there's having Mam and Donal nearby.'

'Donal?'

'My mam's er, manfriend. He's a lovely fella.'

'Well, take it from me, having family nearby makes life easier,' Becca said. 'Especially when you're on your own. It's the little things like when the traffic's bad and I'm running late for the school pick-up, that sort of stuff. It's why I moved to Howth when Gerry and I split.' She shrugged. 'It's not exactly how I saw my life panning out, moving back in with my mam at the ripe old age of thirty-nine, but my dad died a few years ago, and Mam had plenty of room in the house. It just made sense, and it means I can save. I'd like to buy a house of our own.'

'Well, Shay and I are renting, but we'd like to buy once we've decided whether or not we want to stay here in Howth. Although with Noah here,' she gestured at the school, 'and the yoga studio, I feel like we've already put down some pretty strong roots.'

'But?'

Again, Roisin thought Becca had read her mind, giving her a half smile. 'But, I must admit it's taking some time getting used to having my mam popping in on me most days after so many years of doing my own thing in England.'

'So she's very helpful like mine, I take it?' Becca twinkled.

'Oh, very helpful,' Roisin grinned.

'Listen, I know you'll be busy with your studio opening next week, but do you fancy grabbing a coffee. I've an appointment at ten,' Becca checked the slim gold watch on her wrist, 'that would give us an hour?'

'I'd love that, thanks.'

'My car's parked just over there.' Becca pointed to the silver sedan and took a step toward it.

Roisin, spotting Philomena in conversation with another parent, decided now was as good a time as any to try and get back on the right foot with the head of the Parent Association. 'Could you hang on two seconds, Becca? I want to apologise to Philomena for the holy show the other morning.'

'Fair play to you, but I'm warning you, Philomena's not the gracious sort. Last year, when her oldest daughter won the spelling bee, she all but broke out the pom poms and did a cheerleading routine at the assembly. Which I'm telling you now wouldn't have been pretty.'

Roisin laughed at the imagery. The woman was little and round and looked a little like Joseph's sister in her voluminous coat of many colours. That or a part-time art teacher with a penchant for pottery.

'I'll see you at the car.' Becca jangled the keys, leaving Roisin to it.

There was no sign of Dennis, the Dentist, but she planned on apologising on Pooh's behalf when she saw him next. You never knew when you might need an emergency root canal or the like, Roisin thought, standing off to one side and waiting for Philomena to finish her conversation. The seconds ticked by, and Roisin, aware Becca was in her car, was about to give up when Philomena finally said cheerio to the other mother. Nancy had begun dancing about and yip-yapping in her direction. If the little dog could talk, Roisin fancied she'd be enquiring where her paramour, Pooh, was this morning.

Philomena tugged at Nancy's leash. 'Shush Nancy.' She glared at Roisin and was about to push past her, but Roisin had waited this long, and she stood her ground.

'Hello there, I'm Roisin. I'm new to the area. I've Noah, who's just started here at the school.'

Philomena's expression was stony, and Roisin waivered but re-minding herself she didn't want to get off to a bad start here in her new home, ploughed on. 'Erm, while I've got you, Philomena, I wanted to apologise for my mam's poodle's behaviour the other morning and put your mind at rest where little Nancy is concerned because she won't be bringing him to school again.'

If Philomena was curious about how she knew her name, she didn't let on as she finally spoke up. 'I'm glad to hear we won't have any repeat performances because from what Miss Dunlop's been telling me, there've been some very curly questions around what that poodle was trying to do to poor Nancy. From what I understand, there's to be a letter coming home asking parents to please inform their children how to play the game of tag correctly, too. A breakaway faction is going around tapping other children on the shoulder. Instead of saying, 'You're it,' they're after shouting, 'You're sexed.' It's not on.'

Roisin tried to look suitably horrified and quash down the bubble of laughter rising alarmingly rapidly up into her throat because Philomena must have been born without a sense of humour. 'Oh dear,' she squeaked.

'Oh dear indeed, and from what I understand, your son is the ring leader.'

Christ on a bike, but this was not going well. 'I'll have a word with him like.' Roisin squirmed.

'Best you do that.' Philomena tugged Nancy's lead. 'Come on, Nancy. We've a petition to be putting together.'

Roisin watched her join a fellow earth mother with a spaniel. She couldn't say she hadn't been warned; Becca had said she was ungracious. She turned away and crossed the road to where Becca was idling the car engine.

'Well, that went well.' Roisin clambered in alongside her. 'Thanks for waiting.'

'Not at all. And, I hate to say I told you so, but I told you so.'

'You did,' Roisin pulled the safety belt across for the short ride into the village and told Becca about Noah being the ringleader of a breakaway playground group. She was gratified when her new friend snorted with laughter as Roisin relayed Philomena's deadpan expression, repeating the latest version of tag's catchphrase.

'You do realise that this will be one of those stories you pull out on Noah's twenty-first, don't you?'

'One of many,' Roisin muttered through gritted teeth.

Chapter Fifteen

B y the time the two women scanned the busy café, Roisin had learned that Becca started late on a Thursday and it was her morning for errands, appointments and in this morning's case, a coffee date. As for Roisin, she knew she should be at the studio working on next weeks classes routines. Her calendar was fully booked which was brilliant but also meant a lot of planning as each class would be different. Then there was checking with the caterers mammy had booked for the party on Saturday afternoon. Oh, and note to self, she needed to be in the studio tomorrow afternoon to let Donal and the lads in. They were setting up their instruments in anticipation of Saturday's party.

Roisin massaged her temples as her mind whirled with everything she needed to do between now and 2pm on Saturday afternoon. Then, as the tantalising aroma of fresh baking and coffee hit her, her last thought was why had she thought it was a great idea to invite her sisters and co, Mammy and Donal along with Shay's mam and dad for a shared breakfast on Saturday morning? Take each step as it comes, Roisin she told herself inhaling and exhaling slowly and deeply. First things, first. Coffee and a chat with a woman she'd already decided she liked very much.

This morning with no Mammy looking over her shoulder, Roisin decided to treat herself to one of the cream slices in the cabinet. She would not be buying an extra one to drop in to her imposter sister in the boutique clothing shop down the way, either she resolved smiling sweetly at the man with the earring and head scarf behind the counter. He really did look like a pirate, Roisin thought paying. All that was missing was a blackened tooth but that would be a little off-putting and a deterrent to buying all that sugary baking. As she made her way over to the only available table, she hoped she wouldn't feel like she was sailing the seven seas seated in amongst all the nautical paraphernalia on display.

Becca wasn't far behind her and Roisin had just finished sucking the excess cream off her finger when she placed the table number down next to the sugar bowl. 'Your pirate fella up there assured me the coffees won't be long and I'm so glad you decided to er, push the boat out with the cream slice, Roisin. Now I don't feel guilty joining you.'

She'd ordered the same Roisin saw as she set her plate down. 'That is so not funny.' Still she laughed at the cheesy boat pun as Becca discarded her coat hanging it on the back of her chair. 'But I do sometimes wish I'd popped a Sea-Legs tablet before I sit down in here.'

This time Becca laughed.

'As for this,' Roisin said pointing to her plate. 'If my mam was around I'd be on that oaty, seedy yoke by the till under the glass cloche. So, I'm making the most of her absence. She thinks I need to convey the right public image for a yoga teacher and cream slices don't fit the bill. Oh, and call me Rosi, Becca. Everybody does except for when I'm in trouble or my mam's telling me what to do, then I'm Roisin.'

'I'm Rebecca when I'm in bother,' Becca smiled. 'And you have to admire Maureen's business acumen Rosi. She wants your studio to succeed. Although, in my opinion there's a time and a place for oats and that's only at breakfast and only in porridge.' As if to prove her point Becca bit into the squidgy pastry.

'I agree.' Roisin watched as Becca putting the slice down traced her finger around the squished-out cream as she'd done a moment earlier, then popped it in her mouth.

'Mm that's hit the spot.' She'd a speck of pastry stuck to her lip. 'So, tell me how did you get into yoga? Was it a lost year in India?'

Roisin laughed. 'No. Nothing that interesting I'm afraid. Although India's on my bucket list. Yoga was just something that took my fancy and I found a studio near where I lived in London when Noah was small. I found it helped me cope, you know made me a better mother and wife. Or, a calmer one at any rate. I suppose it gave me an hour that was mine and mine alone.' She shrugged. 'I don't know how I'd have survived without it when my marriage imploded. Yoga is my spiritual equivalent of attending daily Mass.' She hoped that didn't sound too wacky not wanting to put Becca off but she didn't seem phased as she deftly polished off the remains of her morning tea.

She spoke through her mouthful. 'And now you're opening your own studio. Well done you.'

'That was the plan at any rate. It doesn't feel like my own studio though.'

'Oh?'

'My mam's supposed to be a silent financial partner only she's not grasped the silent part of our arrangement.'

'Ah, I see.'

They both looked up and smiled their thanks as their coffees arrived and once the piratey man had gone Becca dumping a generous teaspoon of sugar in her coffee and stirring nodded toward Roisin's untouched slice. 'You'd want to eat that because if you don't I won't be responsible for my actions. It was gorgeous.'

Roisin laughed and dutifully bit into the creamy deliciousness.

"I don't care what anyone says about sugar being white poison. It always make me feel better.'

Roisin, oblivious to her cream moustache, nodded her agreement.

'So how did you go from taking classes to teaching them?' Seeing Roisin frantically chew, swallow and wipe her mouth with a paper serviette Becca grinned, 'Sorry it's twenty questions I know.'

'You're grand. I wanted to be able to help people the way, Harriet's Studio where I used to go, had helped me through a tough time. It's incredibly healing, yoga. So, I decide to go for my training certificate in Hatha yoga not long after I split with Noah's dad.'

'You were in London?'

'Uh-huh and once I'd begun the training it became this distant dream to open my own studio.'

'I've heard yoga's great for the mind as well as the body but I've never tried it. I'm looking forward to having a go next week.'

'Well, I hope I can make you a convert.'

'You never know. I could do with the healing,' Becca said somewhat cryptically and then glanced down toward her midriff, 'And some work on that.' When she didn't elaborate further Roisin carried on talking.

'I did my training through Harriet, my teacher, and taught the odd class but the bulk of them are in the evening and that didn't work so well with Noah.'

'What about your ex?'

'He had Noah alternate weekends and I'd put my name down to teach a class then. In the week I was working as a secretary.' Roisin's expression was rueful. 'To be fair, I think I was the world's worst secretary with the world's most tolerant boss. I'm far too much of a dreamer for admin. Then I met Shay and any spare time I had when

Noah was with his dad and Shay was in London, I wanted to spend with him.'

'And now you've set up home together in Howth. What does he do by the way?'

'He coordinates music festivals and plays fiddle in a band that does the rounds of the pubs, The Sullivans, they always get the crowd on the dance floor. I wanted them to play at the studio opening on Saturday but Mammy had already asked Donal, and his band to play. They'll be doing five or so numbers. The party won't drag on into the evening.'

'I'm sensing a musical vibe in your family,' Becca laughed raising her cup to her lips.

'That's a loose way to describe it, Roisin grinned back. 'Donal is the lead singer in a Kenny Roger's tribute band and Mam duets with him on a couple of old hits. She plays the tambourine too. I blame Stevie Nicks for that. She always fancied herself as her whirling about on the stage banging a tambourine like.'

'So I can expect The Gambler and Coward of the County on Saturday with a tambourine solo from your mammy to Edge of Seventeen.'

'Edge of seventy more like but yes, you can indeed.'

Becca was grinning. 'Well, who doesn't love a bit of Kenny?'

'Don't forget Dolly, Sheena and Stevie.' Roisin sipped her drink.

'I won't. I'm looking forward to the party even more now.'

'Thanks, I can guarantee it will be lively.'

'I could do with a spot of livening up. So come on then, tell me more about your Shay.'

'Shay? Well, he's great. I mean really great.' Roisin found herself opening up in a way she never had with someone she barely knew before. There was something about Becca that put her at ease though. 'He's nearly ten years younger than me.'

'Ooh you're a cougar. I like your style sister.'

Roisin laughed. 'I don't feel like one although I was wary of the age gap between us initially, but it was never a problem for Shay. I thought his mam might disapprove when she first met me but she's very much of the attitude if I make Shay happy then she's happy. And he makes me more than happy. He makes me feel complete. He loves Noah too. They've got a great bond. I'm thanking my lucky stars how things are panning out because when my ex announced he was moving to Dubai I was worried it would give Noah all sorts of rejection issues.' Roisin confided how her husband in his wisdom, which had proved to be more arrogance had lost their home through bad investments. The result of this had seen her and Noah move to a small flat while he'd moved home to his mother.

'Now he's run off to the Emirates on his eternal quest to hit the big time financially which he seems to feel is his due. Never mind about Noah and the fact he'll be lucky to see his dad six times a year. Although the flipside of that is I've been able to move back to Ireland and in with Shay.' Roisin took a thoughtful sip of her coffee looking over the cup's rim as she added,

'But given all the changes he's had lately Noah's adjusted to his new life here in Howth well. If you don't count him being the ringleader of the new sexed-tag game that is!'

Becca laughed, 'Don't worry about that. Philomena isn't happy unless there's something she's taking umbrage with. So the only fly in the ointment so to speak is your mam because, and I hope you don't mind me saying this, but from where I'm sitting your life sounds pretty damn good.'

'It is and I sound like a proper un-grate don't I?'

'No. I don't mean it like that but I'm thinking you need to set some clear boundaries when it comes to Maureen's input at the studio. It's your dream after all not hers.'

'I know. You're right but it's easier said than done because her heart's in the right place and I don't want to upset her. Not when she's helped me so much.' Roisin's sigh was weighty and she rewound to the beginning to give Becca a clearer understanding of where she was coming from. 'This studio is important to me on so many levels. I never did anything much, other than flit around London temping, that's how I met Colin. Getting pregnant with Noah wasn't planned and I don't think I'd have married Colin the Arse as my sisters call him if it wasn't the safest option. The easy option. Then when we split up, I'd no choice but to stand up and take charge of my life because it wasn't just about me anymore. I had Noah. I think the divorce was the kick up the arse I needed. Because back then I was a pushover, Easy Osi Rosi, my family used to call me.'

'You don't strike me as a pushover,' Becca interjected. 'Except maybe when it comes to your mam.'

'Point taken.' Roisin's grin was wry. She couldn't take offense because Becca was right. 'I've thought long and hard about that though and I don't think I was easy going so much as I had no confidence in my own judgment.

'They say confidence comes with age.'

Roisin smiled. 'I think that's true to a point. Life throws all sorts of unexpected stuff at you and you've no choice but to develop a backbone. That's why this studio was so important to me. It was a chance to prove to myself that I'm capable of anything if I set my mind to it. Only it turns out I'm not because I couldn't do it without my mam's help. I thought I'd changed but I haven't. I'm still the same Easy Osi Rosi after all. I wish I'd run with my original idea of hiring a room at the community centre and running a couple of classes a week. Keeping things simple, like. Or going to the bank and trying to get a loan. Instead, I took the easy option and Mam's handout.'

Becca put her cup down in the saucer. 'You're being way too hard on yourself, Rosi. And I'm not really in a position to be telling anyone else what to do not given I'm a woman fast approaching forty living under my mammies roof.'

'We're a right pair, aren't we.' Roisin rustled up a smile. 'And I've done nothing but talk about myself since we got here.' The unspoken invitation for Becca to confide in Roisin hung in the air.

'You might regret asking,' Becca finally spoke up.

Roisin shook her head. 'No I won't.'

'Well don't say I didn't warn you.'

It was the second time that morning Becca had said this Roisin thought as she leaned back in her seat to listen.

'I thought I had a great life. I mean I had a lovely home in Rathmines, a handsome husband providing for me and of course Lottie. I hadn't worked since she was born.' Her voice trailed off as she studied the salt and pepper shakers. 'Lottie was already four by the time I convinced Dev, that's my ex, to start trying for another baby. I'd been off the pill for eight or so months and nothing was happening, time was ticking by and I started making noises about tests. Dev was reluctant and that should have been a red flag but I put it down to male pride and put myself through a battery of exams and tests all of which came back clear. Anyway to cut a long story short, I found out through a friend of his who let slip when he'd had a few too many a couple of Christmas's ago that Dev had had a vasectomy a year after Lottie was born. I was never going to get pregnant.'

Roisin gasped and her hand automatically shot across the table nearly knocking the salt over in the process. She set her hand down on top of Becca's wanting to offer comfort. 'I'm so sorry.'

'Don't be it's not your fault.'

'But to let you hope month after month and then go through all those tests.' Roisin shook her head.

'It gets worse, Rosi,' Becca said softly.

Roisin wasn't sure how it could get any worse.

'I couldn't forgive him for what he'd done and rather than inflict actual bodily harm on him I took Lottie and hotfooted it here to Howth, to my mam's. It was only going to be temporary until the divorce was finalised and then I could take my share from the sale of the house and start again.' Becca couldn't meet Roisin's gaze. 'I'm embarrassed to even tell you this next part.'

'Don't be. I'm a judgement free zone, I promise you.'

Becca gave her a tentative smile. 'I've not told anyone this other than my mam because I feel so stupid. I signed things when Dev and I got married. Things I should have got independent legal advice on before I put my name to them but you know how it goes. I was madly in love. Dev and I were solid. We'd be together forever. I trusted him. Anyway it turns out that when the divorce dust settled I wasn't entitled to feck all. Dev's still in what was our home, only his new girlfriend, Grasping Grainne, has since moved in and somewhere along the way he's had his vasectomy reversed because she's six months pregnant. I could almost stomach all of that if it weren't for the fact he's dragging me through the courts trying to get custody of Lottie. Now, suddenly he wants to play happy families and cut me out of that equation.'

'Oh, Becca.' The cream was curdling in Roisin's stomach. She was grateful she'd held back on mentioning her baby plans with Shay. Her grumblings about her mam wielding her influence over the studio seemed pathetic by comparison with what Becca had to deal with.

'He won't get custody. My lawyer's confident of that but in the meantime the legal fees are sucking up the little I did receive when our divorce was settled which is why Lottie and I are still living with my mam. And I should be grateful because we've upended her life and she's been very good about it but honest to God, Rosi if she tells me the correct way to peel an egg or clean around the bathroom tap, or, or—'

'I know exactly what you mean. And you feel awful for feeling,'

'Like an un-grate,' Becca finished.

'Snap.'

They sat in silence for a few seconds until Roisin drained her cup then raising her eyebrows said, 'Grasping Grainne?'

'Colin the Arse?'

They both fell about laughing and Roisin thought it was just as well the café wasn't licenced because she'd a feeling if there'd been a glass of wine on hand she and Becca would have knocked them back with a cheers to new friendships.

Several heads turned to look at the two women wheezing and carrying on at the table over there and then catching sight of the time on her wrist watch, Becca pulled herself together. 'That went so fast. I've got to run.'

'Me too. I'll catch you on Saturday?'

'I wouldn't miss it.' Becca hummed the opening intro to Edge of Seventeen and winked then, she was gone.

Chapter Sixteen

'Oh, do stop complaining, Ralph,' Sienna Burton-Harris's voice trilled down the stairs. It was followed by thudding, thumping, and mutterings about second-rate establishments and the lack of a Bellhop.

Bronagh bristled and polished off her custard cream, brushing the evidence off her lap as the disagreeable couple's voices got closer. She'd be glad to see the back of these two. Ralph Burton-Harris had settled his bill after breakfast. He hadn't wanted to wait for the computer to print off his itemised receipt, so Bronagh had promised to have it waiting for him at reception when he checked out. Now, she folded it in readiness to hand it over. Those who knew her well would recognise that the two red spots on either cheek were a sign she was annoyed by the disparaging comments about the guesthouse she presided over. They'd also wonder if she was suffering from constipation so tight was the smile she bestowed on the Burton-Harris's as they appeared in reception.

Mother of God, what did the woman have on her head? Was it a poor dead rabbit? Bronagh recoiled, swallowing the shocked gasp, but she summoned the strength to take a second peek, and her shoulders returned to normal. It was one of those furry Cossack hat yokes. She half expected yer woman there to fold her arms across her chest, crouch down, and begin the leg-kicking dance moves. It's Dublin you're in, not Siberia, she thought as Sienna Burton-Harris, not bothering to acknowledge her, moved to stand by the door, tapping her foot as she waited for her husband. Well, Bronagh had no wish to hold him up. The sooner they were out that door and, on their way, the better. 'There we are, Mr Burton-Harris.'

His face was florid from the exertion of carting his and his wife's bags down the stairs, and he nearly blinded her, flashing his gold cufflinks about as he tucked the paper away in his wallet. No doubt the stingy gobshite would be claiming their accommodation as an expense no matter if they'd been in Dublin for his uncle's funeral, Bronagh thought. Her face ached with the effort of smiling because she prided herself on being a professional. Nor would he leave a tip. The Irish might not be a nation of tippers but still, and all a monetary offering did take the sting out of putting up with arses like these two. Through gritted teeth, she trotted out a perfunctory, 'I hope you've enjoyed your stay and,' but before she could complete her sentence, there was a loud sniff from the direction of the door while Ralph Burton-Harris's expression was putting her in mind of her recent trip to Santorini for Patrick O'Mara's wedding to Cindy. Little Noah's face had scrunched up like yer man there's, when he'd inadvertently popped an olive in his mouth, thinking it was a grape. 'And I hope we'll see you at O'Mara's again soon. Your taxi should be here any minute.' She dismissed him by pretending to get busy tip-tapping on the computer keyboard. On the screen in front of her, 'eejit, arse, eejitty-arse, arse' blinked back at her.

Ralph Burton-Harris was oblivious to her insincere tone of voice. With a final withering glare, he left his bags where he'd dumped them in front of Bronagh's desk to go and stand alongside his wife by the door.

It took Bronagh three 'ahems' to realise they were waiting for her to open the door. Not only that, but they expected her to carry their bags. Well, they could think on! Because that was not in her job description. Although she'd not have a problem doing so for most of their guests. Then again, most guests would never expect her to cart their bags for them. Where these two were concerned, however, her bottom might as well have been glued to the seat of her ergonomic swivel chair. Nor had she budged by the time the taxi pulled up. It tooted several times before the driver nearly knocked Ralph Burton-Harris over as he pushed open the door to the guesthouse to see where his passengers were.

The driver held the door, and the couple stomped to the taxi. He eyed their bags, then hefting them up, said, 'They better be good tippers.'

Bronagh didn't fancy his chances. 'I'd be taking them the long way to the airport if I were you.'

She was still muttering about rude arses with eejitty hats when Mrs Flaherty appeared fifteen minutes or so later. She'd put her coat on, ready for the off. 'Are you on about those posh gobshites that were staying in Room Six? Because I've not long had Ita in my ear about them not bothering to leave her a tip.'

'The Burton Harris's. Yeah. They'd give you a pain where you should have pleasure those too.'

'You won't hear any argument from me.'

'Was it a busy breakfast service this morning?' Bronagh ventured, trying to gauge the breakfast cook's mood.

'Flat out I was.' Polly's hands ached, but she kept them tucked away in her coat pockets.

Bronagh didn't doubt she'd have heard about it if there had been but asked anyway. 'There's been no more night-time visits from the little red fox since the other morning, then?'

'No.' It was true enough. There had been no further nocturnal visits, but only because Polly had tossed him leftovers the last two mornings. She'd enjoyed having a confidante who didn't offer platitudes or useless advice like John Joseph and his ridiculous remark that she take up handicrafts. The little red fox wouldn't tell her that perhaps it was time to call it a day here at the guesthouse, so Polly kept her counsel on what was on her mind despite Aisling's efforts to get to the bottom of it the other morning. Of course, she didn't let Bronagh know she and her former nemesis had come to an understanding. A private arrangement whereby the fox wouldn't knock the bin over, and he'd receive the breakfast leftovers in return for not leaving a trail of rubbish across the courtyard. Polly, meanwhile, would share all her woes with him. No. If she were to confide any of this in Bronagh, she'd think she'd been inhaling too much bacon fat or the like.

'That's good then.'

'Well, I'll be off now. Things to do. People to see.' Now, that was a blatant fib, but Bronagh didn't need to know that either, Polly thought, making her way toward the door. 'I'll be seeing you tomorrow then.'

'Just a moment, Mrs Flaherty. I almost forgot. You received your invitation to Roisin's party on Saturday afternoon, for the yoga studio like?' Bronagh's hand went to her Cleopatraesque hair. She'd an appointment with a box of Clairol between now and then to touch up her roots. Maureen had informed her that the dress code was a top of her choice, teamed with Mo-pants. She'd be supplied with a pink Bendy Yoga Ladies jacket on arrival. The Mo-pants would be a blessing because she would be taking the pencil skirts she favoured for work off on Friday evening with no intention of revisiting them until Monday morning.

It was Lennie's fault that her skirts made her feel like she was wearing a Victorian-era corset around her tummy. Lennie and the menopause. He had a sweet tooth, did her Lennie and no understanding of the phrase 'a moment on the lips, a lifetime on the hips.' She smiled without being aware she was at the thought of her dear man. It was only five days until he'd be here in Dublin again. Mrs Flaherty was nodding, she realised, asking, 'Will you be coming?'

'I don't think so. It's not my cup of tea, the yoga. Sure, it's for the young wans.'

'Ah, but that's where you're wrong, Mrs Flaherty. I've booked myself into Roisin's Saturday morning classes for the following weekend. She's running a ten o'clock session catering specifically for women who've passed a certain milestone birthday. And you know I've heard it's supposed to be wonderful for the joints like. Roisin was after telling me to think of yoga as being for your joints what an oil change is for a car. I think it will be grand, and of course, there's the free jacket.'

That caught Polly's attention. She was partial to freebies. Who wasn't?

'They're free for family, including O'Mara's longest-serving staff members.' Bronagh referred to herself and Mrs Flaherty. 'Otherwise, you only receive a pink Bendy Yoga Ladies jacket when you purchase a year's subscription.'

Polly's hand rested on the door handle.

'And there's the free drinks, one drink for those that aren't family and nibbles. It's not just potato crisps on offer, either. I'm talking proper nibbles, and The Gamblers are after playing. It's sure to be good craic.'

A jacket, a glass or two and afternoon tea all laid on! Polly could feel herself being swayed. She liked a bit of Kenny, too. 'So, there won't be any actual yoga? It's to be more of a party?'

'Roisin will talk about what she's going to offer in terms of classes, I expect, but unless she's set her routine to Coward of the County, I can't see it.' Bronagh, sensing weakness, dropped her Ace. 'I was thinking you and I could take the DART to Howth, the studios not even a five-minute walk from the station. That way, if we fancy helping ourselves to a second glass, we don't have to worry about driving. And you know yourself it would mean the world to Roisin to have you there.'

Polly would feel badly letting Roisin down. She turned the door-knob, sure where was the harm? The Mister would be playing the bowls. She'd only be rattling around at home. 'I suppose we could go together, and catching the DART makes sense. Sure, you only need to sniff a glass of wine these days to be over the limit, and we wouldn't be expected to join in on any yoga malarkey, you say?'

'Definitely not.'

'Well, I don't see why not then.'

'I'll look forward to it.'

To her surprise, as she left the guesthouse, Polly realised she'd a little spring in her step.

Chapter Seventeen

♥

Roisin and Shay hadn't wanted to hold a housewarming party because one Howth housewarming in the family was more than enough in their lifetime. Donal and Mammy's hoolie in their new home was still too fresh in everyone's minds for a repeat performance. Roisin had pointed this out when her sisters had asked whether they could expect an official invitation to the new house anytime soon. She'd told them she had no energy to organise anything besides the Bendy Yoga Studio opening.

Roisin originally envisaged gathering close friends and family to celebrate the launch of her new business venture. Somehow, along the way, it had expanded into a 'grand opening' with everyone from the bin man to elderly pedestrians with a penchant for little red sausages invited for drinks and nibbles. Really, it was just as well Mammy was putting her hand in her pocket to spring for it. She'd hate to think what the food and drinks bill would be.

In the end, it was fear of her sisters deciding to take matters into their own hands and organise a surprise that saw Roisin blurt out, 'Why don't you come over for a family breakfast on the morning of the studio opening instead? Sure, I won't have much time with you at the party in the afternoon, but all of us sitting around the kitchen table together breaking bread would be a grand start to the day.' She still didn't know where that had come from!

'And will you be saying Grace and all before you break the bread, like?' Moira had asked tartly.

Aisling had suggested making it a shared breakfast because she didn't want to sit around a table eating nothing but bread. Thanks very much. After all, she was breastfeeding two babies, and a slice of Brennan's family pan wouldn't cut the mustard. Given everything she'd have to do that day, Roisin hadn't argued, grasping hold of the shared breakfast idea and running with it. Once Moira got over her snit about having to bring something other than herself, Tom and the toddler Kiera, they'd all agreed it was a grand idea, even Mammy. Although she'd taken a day longer to get over her snit because the shared family breakfast hadn't been her idea.

Now, the day was finally here. Today, she officially opened the Bendy Yoga Studio! 'Pinch me,' Roisin murmured, needing to know she wasn't dreaming.

'I will Mummy.'

'Ow! Noah!' Still and all, it was confirmation she was wide awake, and rubbing her arm, she gazed out the kitchen window, scanning the sky. The patches of blue were a good omen, she decided, swinging around to slap Noah's hand away from where he'd been about to help himself to yet another watermelon cube from the chopped fruit platter that was Roisin's contribution. 'You can't just pick out the pieces you like, Noah.'

'Why not?' His little face was genuinely puzzled. 'I only like the watermelon, the green and orange one tastes like poo.'

'Yeah, why not?' Shay, whisking eggs for the French toast he intended to whip up, looked over his shoulder with a wink at Roisin.

She'd deal with him later, Roisin thought, smiling inwardly. 'Please don't say poo or sexed today, Noah. Those words are off limits, and if you promise me not to say them, you can have one more piece of the watermelon, but that's it.'

Noah's hand hovered over the platter like a fly. 'How long am I not allowed to say poo or sexed for?'

Roisin could see Shay's shoulders shaking, and struggled to keep a straight face.

'For good. Thanks very much. I never want to hear those words again. Do you hear me?' God, she sounded like her mam sometimes. Next, she'd be asking him if his ears were painted on.

'Well, Mummy, that calls for at least three pieces of watermelon, don't you think?'

Her son was destined for a glorious career in politics, Roisin decided fetching a plate and putting three cubes of the red fruit on it. She held it out of reach until they'd shaken on the deal. Happy, Noah carted his plate through to the front room, and she heard the blare of the Saturday morning cartoons but didn't have the heart to shout at him to turn the volume down.

Ten minutes and they'd be here, Roisin saw, glimpsing at the microwave clock and feeling an anticipatory flutter. Well, she was as ready for today as she'd ever be. All she had left to do was change into her new wintergreen top after they'd eaten. She'd never hear the end of it if she got egg yolk or the like down the front of it.

Surprisingly, Roisin had slept soundly the night before. This she put down to knowing everything that could be done to ensure this afternoon's party went off without a hitch had been done. The caterers had assured her they'd be providing enough in the way of finger food to feed those who'd RSVP'd as well as the blow-ins they were expecting thanks to Mammy inviting anyone with a pulse, and yes, they'd added cocktail sausages and sausage rolls to the offerings.

Yesterday afternoon, Noah and his new friend Olwyn, who was a tad too worldly for Roisin's liking, had joined her at the studio where they'd been tasked with making paper chains. Meanwhile, Donal, Mammy and Shay put their puff into the colourful balloons hanging in bunches from the ceiling. The Gamblers, instruments in tow, had almost trooped up the stairs without incident to set up in the corner Mammy had decided had the best acoustics. Almost, but not quite. Unfortunately, Rosemary was crushed by Davey's drum kit. He'd not seen her because he did not have his glasses on, and his vision was further impaired because of the kit he was carrying. He was oblivious right up to the moment Rosemary thunked into the studio, clutching her ribs and muttering on about near-death experiences with drum kits. To quieten her down, Mammy insisted Davey apologise for skewering her to the wall, then set her to work polishing the glasses they'd hired and lining them up on the trestle table. Cathal, Rosemary had explained once she could speak properly, had a run-on heel repairs and couldn't join them.

Mammy even had a red ribbon she insisted Roisin cut before anyone stepped over the studio threshold, she'd announced as Roisin locked up. Roisin realised this was over the top, but secretly, she was thrilled with the idea of a ribbon-cutting ceremony.

Now, she smiled at the thought of the day ahead and moving alongside Shay, she peered over his shoulder to watch what he was doing.

'Now for the secret ingredient.' He sprinkled cinnamon in the egg mix and whisked it before setting the bowl aside. 'Excited?'

Her nervous energy must be coming off her in waves, Roisin thought. 'Anxious as to how it will go today but mostly excited and very happy.'

'Glad to hear it, and don't be anxious,' he kissed the tip of her nose. 'Just enjoy your special day. You deserve this, Rosi. I'm super proud of you.'

Unexpected tears pricked because his words meant so much. 'I'm proud of you' wasn't a sentiment Roisin had heard much in her life. Oh, Mammy and Daddy had clapped the loudest at school assemblies. They told her she was brilliant when she got the certificate for effort or always being on time. Still, even then, Roisin had known those certificates were token gestures. And yes, Mammy and Daddy would have been proud of her no matter what. Well, maybe not so much if she were a criminal, but she was getting off point. The thing was, this studio was something she was proud of herself.

Shay wasn't going to give her a chance to get emotional or ruin her makeup, which she'd taken an age to apply, because before she could so much as blink, he pulled her to him, pressing his mouth down on hers. Roisin was just beginning to wish they'd another half hour until the family arrived and could nip upstairs while Noah was engrossed in the television when a sudden sharp rapping at the window saw them spring apart like naughty teenagers caught having a fumble.

'Jaysus.' Roisin shook her head, seeing Moira's hand to her forehead, nose pressed to the glass, glaring at them, looking for all the world like a prudish nun. A prudish nun who bore an uncanny resemblance to Demi Moore. 'The face on her. You'd think she was the virgin bride.'

Shay laughed and flicked the tea towel over his shoulder, switching the elements on to heat the pan as Roisin pointed in the direction of the door, not waiting for Moira's nod of understanding as she went to answer it.

'Sorry! I never heard you knocking over the television. Come in, come in.' Roisin, a welcome smile plastered to her face, oblivious to the lipstick smeared Joker-like around her mouth thanks to Shay, stepped aside, holding the door open wide. Aisling proffered her cheek for a hello kiss and then raised the hip with Aoife balancing on it so Roisin could do the same for her niece, jiggling the other for Connor to be greeted. Then, she stared at her sister.

'Roisin, it's only Mammy who's mastered the art of putting the lipstick on without a mirror, you know that.' She shook her head, hair a cascade of burnished copper, unaware of the streak of Roisin's lippy on her cheek.

In honour of the occasion, she was wearing her Mo-pants, Roisin noticed and a super-snug top that was bound to start Noah harping on again about his school trip last year and the cows he'd seen being milked. She rolled her eyes in anticipation.

Aisling glimpsing her babies', plump, soft branded cheeks, made noises about how that better come off, as she pushed past her sister and followed her nose to the kitchen.

Next, Quinn appeared bearing an enormous tray of sticky cinnamon scrolls wedged next to one another. 'Homemade,' he said proudly as Roisin repeated the lipstick smearing.

'They look and smell divine, Quinn. You may enter.'

'Thanks. I'll have to pop back out once I've deposited this to fetch the baby bag and their bouncers.'

Mammy was often heard to lament it was a miracle any baby had made it through to adulthood in days of old without a truckload of paraphernalia being carted about wherever they went.

'Tesco's home brand!' Tom sprang up, holding up a loaf of bread. 'Moira said it would be useful for the toast like and that I was to tell you we're both students in case you'd forgotten.' His eyes twinkled. His other hand had a firm hold of the toddler Kiera. Her thumb was in her mouth, and her face was nearly hidden by the manky blanket she was snuffling. 'She fell asleep in the car,' Tom said as he was marked with long-lasting lippy.

'Hello, sweetheart.' Roisin crouched down so she was at eye level with her niece. 'Noah's in the front room watching the cartoons. Why don't you go and join him?'

Kiera loved Noah, and still clutching her bedraggled blankie, she tugged her hand free from her daddy's, but before she could trot off inside, Roisin grabbed her in a hug that made her giggle. Then, she gave her niece the requisite kiss.

Roisin straightened, and Kiera tottered inside. 'Noah, turn that television down,' she hollered over her shoulder, inadvertently shouting in Quinn's face. 'Sorry about that.'

Blinking in shock, Quinn rubbed his ears and headed out for his second load.

For once, Roisin's shouting had an effect, and to her amazement, she could hear herself think as her son obligingly turned the volume down.

'Mummy says I'm not to say the poo or sexed word alright Kiera.'

Jaysus wept! 'Do you want me to take that for you?' Roisin relieved Quinn of one of the baby bouncers and was about to close the door behind them when Moira shot around from the side of the house. She'd forgotten all about her younger sister! 'What took you so long?'

'My heels got stuck in the mud,' she explained as Roisin hugged and kissed her and finally closed the door.

'Mammy and Donal here?' Moira asked.

'Not yet.'

Aisling's voice floated forth from the depths of the kitchen. 'You better not be wearing my Dior's again, Moira. Or there'll be murder.'

Moira looked furtive and slipped the muddied heels off, leaving them by the front door. 'Rosi, you might want to wipe your face before Mammy, and Donal arrive. You look like you were just after having a quick one.'

'Thanks a million, and no chance of that with you getting about peeping in windows,' Roisin muttered, wiping around her mouth.

The coffee was brewed when Jodie and Phillip, Shay's parents, breezed in bearing brioche rolls and a bunch of enormous flowers for Roisin. They were quickly enfolded into the family fray. Just as Shay flipped the last piece of French toast, a breathless Maureen and Donal fronted up. Maureen was an Arpège scented vision in wintergreen. At the same time, Donal was Kenny's doppelganger in his white suit and open-necked shirt.

'Patrick was after telephoning,' Maureen gushed by way of explanation. 'And I was so busy listening to him telling me how his doctor's after saying he thinks he's experiencing sympathetic Braxton-Hicks contractions that I burned the egg and bacon flan. Donal had to race to the supermarket and pick up a Quiche Lorraine. He was lucky to get it. It was the last one, and he had a tug-o-war beside the frozen foods for it with a woman who fancied quiche for lunch, but when he explained what had happened to my flan, she gave in and let him have it.'

'She's after having a pork pie for lunch instead,' Donal added.

'And did our lovely brother happen to mention how Cindy's doing?' Aisling asked, eyebrow arched as she rocked a cooing Aoife's bouncer with her foot.

'Oh, sure, she's grand.' Maureen flapped her hand dismissively.

'Thanks Donal. I know you fought hard for this.' Roisin grinned, took the quiche from him, and set it on the table. She was about to lunge in for a hello kiss when Maureen shrieked.

'Don't you be going near Donal with that muck on your face, Roisin! Not when he's wearing his best white Kenny suit.'

Roisin took a step back from Donal hands in the air.

'Sweet Mother of Divine, Roisin!' Maureen said, giving herself a pat down, trying to locate her glasses about her person.

'They're on your head, Mo,' Donal supplied.

Maureen gave him a doe-eyed look of gratitude and, slipping them on, peered through the lens at her eldest daughter. 'Who do you think you are with all that lipstick on your face? Is it Jezabel herself you're after impersonating?' Then, one by one, Maureen took stock of the faces filling the kitchen, 'And are you lot her followers?' Her brown eyes finally rested on the youngest members of the family. 'Oh, my poor grand-babbies. Look what you've done to them, Roisin.'

Aisling came to the rescue with wet wipes, which were hastily passed around.

'It's yer Boots woman. She's after doing the hard sell on the long-lasting lipstick,' Roisin mumbled, letting Shay wipe her face clean before she did his. Popping the quiche in the oven to warm it through, she thought she'd have to smarten herself up again before she left for the studio.

Shay began playing the host with the most as he passed out the Bellinis he'd made earlier and the non-alcoholic version he'd made for those who didn't tipple. When everyone had a glass, Maureen cleared her throat, and Roisin braced for a speech, but Shay beat her to it.

This time, as he told her sisters, their partners, his mam and dad, and her mam and Donal how proud he was of what Roisin had achieved, she couldn't stop the fat tear rolling down her cheek. She already looked like Ronald McDonald. She thought she might as well add streaked mascara into the mix, sniffing. How she wished her late daddy was here. He would have loved Shay, and looking at her sisters, she could see they were missing him, too.

'To Roisin!' A chorus of voices sounded, followed by much glass clinking, and finally, they all took a sip of the peachy cocktails.

'Now can we eat?' Aisling demanded, gesturing to the table. 'This all looks amazing, and I'm starving.'

'Fading away so you are,' Moira said under her breath, receiving a glare from her sister.

'Quinn and I need sustenance to revive us. Thanks very much. We're after having a terrible night's sleep.'

'The twins teething?' Roisin enquired sympathetically, able to recall the broken night's sleep and unsettled days of Noah's formative years as she pulled a chair out for Shay's mam.

'No. I was after having a nightmare about Bono. He performed at your grand opening this afternoon but refused to sing anything other than 'I Still Haven't Found What I'm Looking For.' I offered to help him bloody well find whatever it was he was after just so that he'd bugger off, but no, he'd start at the beginning and sing it all over again. I woke up in a terrible sweat.'

'Why didn't Quinn get a good night's sleep?' Donal piped up.

'Because he thought I was after having a naughty dream and he'd try his luck, only I was still half asleep and thought he was Bono, so I kicked him.'

All eyes turned to Quinn, and there were empathetic murmurings.

'It really hurt too,' he said, limping around the table to his spot milking the sympathy vote.

'It's very quiet in that front room. Tom, you should go and check.' Moira bossed, already pulling a chair out to sit down. 'Tell Noah and Kiera to come through and have something to eat.'

Roisin and Shay had borrowed plastic outdoor chairs from the neighbours. As promised, Donal had brought the fold-out picnic seats, and soon, everyone, children included, had a pew around the table.

'So, are you excited, Roisin?' Jodie enquired.

'Excited, nervous.' Roisin's smile was tremulous.

'You'll be grand.'

'She will.' Shay smiled at his mam and squeezed Roisin's hand under the table.

'Did I tell you I'm after arranging for the local papers to be there to photograph the event?'

'Ah, no, Mammy, I don't want to be on the paper's front page in my Mo-pants. I haven't got my pre-baby body back yet,' Aisling wailed.

'It's not about you, Aisling. This is your sister's day.'

Roisin listened to the bickering and bantering around the table as they tucked into their feast. This was what it was all about, she thought, smiling. Family.

The toddler, Kiera, began banging her spoon on the table, looking a sight with lipstick and sticky cinnamon sugar smeared across her face. In seconds, she'd even managed to get tomato sauce in her hair.

'What would you like, Kiera. Nana will get it for you?'

Kiera gave her nana her biggest, brightest, most cherubic smile and said, 'Sexed, poo.'

Roisin remembered the quiche as the smell of burning hit her nostrils.

Burnt quiche and toddlers using rude words! What next?

Chapter Eighteen

♥

A crowd was gathering at the top of the lane way leading to The Bendy Yoga Studio and the air was filled with excited chatter. Beneath her feet Roisin fancied she could feel the faint vibration of the DART rumbling into the station and overhead seagulls squawked hopeful of the visitors it was about to disgorge tossing them the odd chip. It was that sort of day after all. A day for making the most of the blue sky by wrapping up and enjoying fish and chips by the seaside. Shay had hold of her hand and Noah was buzzing around upstairs with Kiera and their Poppa D as they called Donal. Her son was under strict instructions not to further corrupt his cousin, Kiera with his vocabulary.

Quinn and Tom were upstairs too, ready to man the bar, and when Mammy last rang up to check, everything was under control they'd assured her the caterers were good to go. The twins were obliging by having fallen asleep in their carrycots. Bless them, Roisin thought. The twins that was, not her brothers-in-law. The pair of them were under strict instructions from Aisling and Moira not to touch a drop while on duty. Personally, Roisin felt the odds of that happening were about the same as Noah managing not to utter his new favourite 'S' word for an entire afternoon.

There was a one drink per person policy and Shay would give the lads a hand with the drinks if it got too hectic because this lot here looked like they'd try it on for seconds. Right now, though Roisin was glad of his solid warmth next to her because seeing all these unfamiliar faces made her want to bite her nails. As if reading her mind he put his arm around her waist.

Meanwhile, her sisters had been sent to the top of the lane by Mammy to assure those unfamiliar with the location of the studio tucked away as it was that they'd found the right place. Given her sign hadn't turned up yet Roisin was grateful to them. A giddy giggle rose up in her throat at the thought of Moira and Aisling's faces once the breakfast things had been cleared away earlier and Mammy had presented them with their Bendy Yoga Ladies pink jackets. Shay's mam Jodie had received one too appearing genuinely chuffed to be included in the yoga girl gang. Unlike her sisters who had tried their hardest to get out of having to wear them.

'But Mammy the pink clashes with my hair,' from Aisling.

'I'm an art student Mammy and you're ruining my image,' from Moira.

Given who it was they were up against it was no surprise they now looked like two bouncers in pink standing on either side of the lane.

Next to her she heard Mammy on her mobile phone. 'How many have we got lined up now Moira?' There was a pause then, 'Who do you think it is? It's your mammy.'

Roisin and Shay grinned at each other because there was nothing stopping Maureen from taking the few short steps up the lane to the main street. She refused however to leave her post guarding the red ribbon strewn across the open door lest anyone make a break for the free savouries and drink waiting for them upstairs.

Seconds later she nudged Roisin. 'Moira's after reporting that the queue is down the street now.'

The fluttering in Roisin's stomach intensified and to distract herself she tugged at her top and turned toward Shay. 'Does the wintergreen go with the pink?'

'Definitely,' Shay answered correctly.

He must be colourblind and this had somehow slipped her attention, Roisin thought knowing full well it was a lie.

'Oh, look who's here.' Maureen waved out and Roisin forgot she was nervous spying Bronagh and Mrs Flaherty elbowing their way down the lane importantly. Goodness was Mrs Flaherty wearing leggings under her coat there? That was a turn up and good for her.

'Out the way please, VIP's coming through,' Bronagh declared. Heads turned toward the voice to see who the guest celebrities were.

'I think I might have seen yer wan with the black hair on Stars in their Eyes. She did a grand Cher. But, I've no clue who the other wan is,' someone was heard to say.

Maureen forgetting she'd hold of the ribbon cutting scissors stepped forward arms held out to greet her old friends.

'She's got scissors!' someone hollered. A panicked jostling ensued but Shay restored calm by assuring the lined-up women that there was nothing to worry about.

'Hasn't he got a fine bottom on him,' a voice sang out.

'I wonder if he's after doing the yoga, like,' came the reply. 'I'll sign up my Frank if so.'

Jaysus wept thought Roisin as she waited her turn to greet Bronagh and Mrs Flaherty.

'Sorry about that.' Maureen said setting the scissors down on the door stoop before hugging her two old friends warmly. 'I've a lovely pink jacket for youse both upstairs. One size fits all.'

Then it was Roisin's turn. 'I'm so glad you both came, thank you.'

'We wouldn't have missed it would we Mrs Flaherty?'

Polly's cheeks looked even more appley than usual as she beamed at Roisin. 'Tis a proud day for all of us who know and love you Roisin.'

Over their shoulders, Roisin spotted Becca at the top of the lane and waved out. The older woman with her must be her mam and she'd brought Lottie with her. Becca waved back and mouthed 'good luck'. Cathal Carrick the cobbler as Roisin always thought of him and Rosemary emerged from the shoe shop. Cathal locked up while Rosemary thunked over to chat to Bronagh and Mrs Flaherty whom she'd met on several different occasions over the years.

Roisin took the opportunity to mentally tot up who had her back here today and the butterflies disappeared knowing she'd her family, Bronagh and Mrs Flaherty included, a new friend and even Rosemary and Cathal Carrick the cobbler were rooting for her to succeed. She was suddenly eager to snip that ribbon and get upstairs to show them and all these other people, potential yoga students each and every one of them, her beautiful new studio. As though reading her mind Mammy made a show of clearing her throat. It had little effect on the chattering women and it was only when Shay clapped his hands that they stood up a little taller and paid attention. Roisin fancied she heard an audible inhaling as the gathered women sucked in their tummies and batted their lashes in his direction.

'Thank you Shay,' Maureen said. It had been decided the meet and greet here would be short and sweet with Roisin giving a proper talk about her hopes for the studio once everybody had a drink and something to eat in hand. 'What a lovely turn out we've got.' Maureen beamed in her applecart now she had everyone's attention. Thank you all for coming today to share in myself and my daughter Roisin's grand Bendy Yoga Studio Opening!'

Applause rippled and echoed around the lane and the street beyond and hearing it Roisin decided to let the reference to the studio being Mammy's as well slide. She was excited was all, and fair play to her, because Roisin knew she wouldn't be standing here now about to cut that red ribbon if not for her help. It would be churlish not to let her share in her moment in the sun.

'So, without further ado, let's cut this ribbon and mark the official opening of,' Maureen spun around flashing the back of her pink jacket, then spun back, 'The Bendy Yoga Ladies Studio!'

The cheering was almost evangelical. Roisin was hopeful of a huge run-on annual subscriptions this afternoon because the pink jacket was clearly a hit. Now where were those scissors? She watched Rosemary who must have picked them up hand them to Mammy and held her hand out expectantly.

Maureen made no move to hand them over as she turned toward the ribbon. 'I thought we could cut it together like, Roisin.'

'Ah no Mammy. Sure there's no need I'm perfectly able to manage a pair of scissors on my own,' Roisin countered playing dumb. 'Pass them over.'

Maureen held tight with a white knuckled grasp. 'I just think it would be a nice touch for us to cut the ribbon together given we're officially partners.'

'Silent partners, Mammy.' Roisin made a grab for the scissors but Maureen held her hand out of reach.

'Come on now Roisin. I didn't raise you to be selfish, like. Wrap your hand around mind and snip-snippety-snip away we go.'

'But Mammy you said it was my ribbon to cut. You heard her didn't you Shay.' She hated sounding petulant like a child but that was precisely how she did feel.

Shay looked torn. On the one hand he desperately wanted to fecky brown nose his way back to being on Maureen's good side after accidentally flashing her in Santorini, but he didn't want to let Roisin down either. He was saved from answering by Maureen butting in.

'But partner's do things together don't they Rosemary?'

Rosemary opened her mouth but neither Maureen or Roisin caught her reply thanks to the disgruntled cry that went up.

'Get on with it! Sure those little red sausages will be after getting cold.'

Roisin recognised the elderly woman, Mammy had invited the other day. She'd a surprisingly strong voice on her for one so little she thought noticing the crowd was getting restless. If they weren't careful the crowd would turn into an angry mob like the French revolution lot outside Versailles. 'Alright Mammy we can cut the ribbon together but my hands go on the bottom.'

'Compromising is a life skill, Roisin.' Maureen nodded graciously and passed the scissors to Roisin.

For a split second Roisin thought about diving for that ribbon and cutting it in half before Mammy knew what was what. Life would not be worth living if she did. So, slipping her fingers through the plastic handles of the scissors, she waited for Mammy to wrap her hands over the top. 'Ready?' she looked into a matching pair of brown eyes.

'Ready.'

Snip, snip, snip and another snip.

'Could you not have found sharper scissors Mammy?'

'Put more elbow into it Roisin.'

Snip. The ribbon fluttered to the ground on either side of the door.

'I declare the Bendy Yoga Studio officially open!' Roisin shouted before her mammy could.

'And so do I!' Maureen added.

Chapter Nineteen

'I'm so glad you could come.' Roisin hugged Becca, mindful of not knocking her glass. Her hair smelled of coconut shampoo. It was gorgeous. She'd have to ask her what brand she used.

'Thanks so much for inviting us,' Becca said when they broke apart, waving her free hand about. The studio looks fantastic, by the way. I've heard so many favourable comments. I can't wait to come along to a class next week!'

'Thanks' Roisin beamed. The fears only Shay had been privy to over the last weeks about no one being interested in joining yoga and her falling flat on her face with this venture had been allayed. The timetable had filled up nicely the closer they got to this afternoon's grand opening, and already this afternoon, a dozen or so women who'd collared her to chat about what classes she had to offer had made bookings. The turnout on the men's part was slimmer. Roisin had well and truly put her foot down over Mammy's idea of Moira parading up and down the main street in sprayed-on Mo-pants inviting every Tom, Dick and Harry along to her men's only mid-week session, though. 'We might as well hang a red light in the window and be done with it, Mammy,' she'd said. It was a relief when she'd conceded that it might send mixed messages about what services were on offer down the little lane. Besides, Donal had reassured them he was doing his best to spread the word at the bowls club, and the rest of The Gamblers had promised to come along to a class.

'I think it's going to be a big success,' Becca assured her.

'I hope so,' Roisin dimpled and then realised she'd not seen her son, Lottie and Kiera. 'You haven't seen where the children got to have you? Last I saw, they'd a plate of food each, but I've no clue where they're now.'

'They're under there.' Becca pointed to the food table covered by a large cloth. 'It's their tent.'

'I don't blame them hiding,' Roisin laughed.

'It's great they're all getting on. Who does the little one belong to, by the way?'

Roisin hoped Becca would still say the same if Lottie went home later with a new word or two in her vocabulary. 'My youngest sister Moira and her partner Tom, who's manning the bar. He's breaking out the Tom Cruise Cocktail moves even though only a glass of fizzy wine is on offer. Next to him is my middle sister, Aisling's husband Quinn, the Ronan Keating lookalike.'

'Phew, I think I got all that.'

'I'll quiz you later on who's who,' Roisin grinned. 'I put Noah in charge of looking out for his cousin Kiera. She's a sweetheart but very determined, like her mammy. I think Moira's finally met her match.'

Becca was still looking toward the busy bar, though. 'I knew yer man up there reminded me of someone! Ronan Keating! Thank you, it was niggling away at me. He's the spitting image. Can he sing?'

'No, but he can cook like. He owns Quinn's Bistro on Baggot Street. Do you know it?'

'The Irish place?'

'That's it.'

'I've not been, but I've heard good things about it.'

'Shay's bands playing there in a couple of weeks. You and I should make a night of it.'

'I'd really like that Rosi. I feel like I've not had a night out in forever.'

Come to think of it, so did Roisin. 'It's a date then.' She would have clinked a glass with Becca's if she'd had one in her hand. 'Have you managed to infiltrate that crowd of Janet the gannets hovering around the food table yet and grab something to eat?'

Becca laughed. 'Oh, don't worry about me. I'm grand Mam sorted that lot out.' She craned her neck, scanning the faces of the milling crowd. 'She's disappeared on me again. I'm trying to keep an eye on her because she's already two-thirds through her second glass, even though I told her there was one complimentary glass on offer on arrival. I'm warning you now, Rosi, three, and she's anyone's!'

So much for one glass per person; Roisin would have a word in Tom and Quinn's ears to pay more attention to the faces they were serving so they didn't ply repeat offenders with more free bubbles than necessary. Sure, look it, there was Bold Brenda, and Roisin was certain, given the rosy glow on her cheeks and predatory gleam in her eyes, she wasn't sitting on her first. 'Do you see that fella over there with the terrified look in his eyes?' The knowing smile on Becca's lips told Roisin she already knew who he was.

'I take it that's your Shay being manhandled by Brenda?'

'You know Brenda?'

'Mam's told me all about her. They're in the rambling group together.'

'Oh, so's my mam or she was. She's been busy with grandchildren lately.' Roisin lowered her voice, 'We call her Bold Brenda, and I think we'd better go and rescue Shay.'

The two women jostled their way over to where Shay was trying to inch away from the woman inching ever closer, but he had nowhere to inch.

'Brenda, it's lovely to see you again,' Roisin greeted.

Relief flashed across Shay's face seeing her.

'Hello there, Roisin. I've not seen you since your mammy and Donal's housewarming party. You're looking well, and so is your handsome young man, Shay. I was just after telling him I've got my dancing shoes on, and with my Niall unable to make it this afternoon, I've reserved a dance with Ol' brown eyes here. 'Lady.' It's a lovely, slow one. Cheek to cheek like.'

The horror that flashed across Shay's face was comical, and Roisin galloped in on her white charger to save him. 'Ah, now Brenda, that's my favourite Kenny song, and you can't be stealing him off me at my own party.'

Brenda's expression said she'd have no qualms in doing so whatsoever, and silently saying sorry to Moira's other half, Roisin added, 'Have you said hello to Tom? You'll remember him from Mam and Donal's housewarming.'

'The barman with the bulging biceps who was good with his hands, like?' Brenda's face lit up. 'He wasn't there when I received my, erm, first glass of bubbles. It was some fella who'd the look of Ronan Keating about him. I prefer a man who's built, you know.'

'He must have been taking a break. He's definitely there now.'

Shay was promptly forgotten as Brenda put her head down like an American footballer and charged for the bar.

'I don't know if I should be insulted over being cast aside so easily,' Shay said, leaning in and kissing Roisin.

'I'd be grateful if I were you,' Becca laughed, holding a hand out. 'I'm Becca. Rosi and I met outside the school gates on Noah's first day. It's nice to meet you.'

'Hi, Shay Redmond and Rosi's told me all about you. It's great you could come along this afternoon.' Shay returned the handshake.

'It's Becca's daughter, Lottie, who Noah and Kiera are camping with under the tablecloth,' Roisin explained.

Becca suddenly dived for a passing woman, bringing her up short. 'Mam, I've been looking for you.'

'You nearly made me spill my wine then, Rebecca. And I'm after mixing and mingling.' She looked past her daughter to where Roisin was standing. 'Oh, hello there. You're Maureen's daughter, aren't you? I'm Becca's mam, Peg.'

Roisin could see where her new friend got her pretty blue eyes from. 'I am. I'm Roisin, Maureen's eldest. My younger sisters are somewhere about.'

'And it's you who's running this place?'

'It is.'

'Because I was after chatting to Rosemary about your Saturday morning classes for women of a certain vintage.'

'You've had too much of a certain vintage, Mam,' Becca growled.

''Tis my first, Becca.'

Her daughter narrowed her eyes.

'As I said before my daughter rudely interrupted. I was having a word with Rosemary about your Saturday morning classes, and I'd like you to put my name down if you still have room.'

'I do, and of course I can.'

'Grand. It's a lovely do you and Maureen are after putting on by the way.'

'I'm glad you're enjoying yourself.'

'Oh, she is,' Becca answered for her.

'Rosi, over here.' Bronagh bobbed about, beckoning her.

'Excuse me. It was lovely to meet you, Peg,' Roisin smiled and pushed her way over to O'Mara's receptionist.

'I've been telling Mrs Flaherty here about the Saturday morning class you're going to be running for women who aren't in their first flush of youth, Roisin.' Bronagh's glass of wine sloshed alarmingly in her glass as she swayed about in her pink Bendy Yoga Ladies jacket.

Mrs Flaherty's eyes had a slightly glazed look to them. She was wearing her new jacket and agreed that this was true.

So much for Mammy's one complimentary glass rule, Roisin thought deciding it wasn't her problem. She'd have been happy to roll with green tea for all. It was clear neither Bronagh nor Mrs Flaherty made a habit of imbibing in the afternoon. 'Have either of you had anything to eat?'

'Cop yourself on Rosi. Have you seen that lot up there?' Bronagh flapped her hand toward the table. A core group of women had formed a semi-circle around it. 'Sure, they're harder than yer protesting Suffragettes back in the day to breach.'

'Fair play. I'll see if I can't pop out to the kitchen and rustle youse both up something.'

'What were we just talking about?' Bronagh squinted at Mrs Flaherty, but Roisin answered. 'The Saturday morning yoga class.'

'Oh yes. I was after trying to talk Mrs Flaherty into coming along with me. Sure, what's the point of wearing the jacket if you won't talk the walk.'

Roisin's mouth twitched. 'Talking the talk if you're not going to walk the walk, Bronagh.'

'That's what I said.'

Roisin looked to Mrs Flaherty.

'But I'm not talking the talk; I'm just wearing the jacket. And a grand jacket it is, too. I'm happy to do my bit wearing it and spreading the word. No offence, Rosi, and I think you've done a grand job with the studio, but like I've already told Bronagh, I don't think yoga's my sort-a thing.'

Remembering her conversation with Aisling about their dear cook not being herself of late, Roisin decided she wouldn't let her off that easy. She thought of all those snaffled rasher sandwiches of her youth, not to mention having a cuddly confidante well out of reach of Mammy and her sisters' flapping ears in the basement kitchen of O'Mara's and dug her heels in. 'I tell you what, Mrs Flaherty. If you come to next Saturday morning's class with Bronagh, I won't charge you a penny, and if you still say yoga's not for you at the end of it, I promise I'll never broach the subject with you again.'

'And neither will I,' Bronagh piped up. 'Now you can't say fairer than that, Mrs Flaherty. And sure, look it, you've the leggings already.'

'It won't be a competition, Mrs Flaherty. It's your body, and you know its limits.'

'Well, I can tell you now, Rosi, it's limited, but I suppose there's no harm in coming along for a look.'

Polly Flaherty would later claim she only agreed because she was under the influence. Still, she was also a woman of her word. She'd not waiver once she'd given it.

From the corner of her eye, Roisin saw her mammy spoon at the ready, glass raised and took a series of calming ujjayi breaths.

'Are you alright there, Roisin,' Polly asked.

'She's grand. She's doing the prani-what-sit breathing,' Bronagh supplied. She enjoyed being in the know when it came to the yoga terms.

'It's speech time,' Roisin murmured. 'I won't forget to fix youse both something to eat after.' She stood alongside her mammy as she gave the spoon and glass a thwack to get the partygoers' attention. The butterflies were back. She wished she hadn't opted to speak off the cuff, but she'd felt it would flow more from her heart. Her palms were clammy, and her stomach jitterbugging as all eyes turned toward her.

Chapter Twenty

♥

'Eh-hem. A little bit of hush, please. My daughter Rosin has a few words she'd like to say.' Maureen puffed up proudly like a pufferfish, as she was prone to doing during such moments.

Before Roisin could say a word, however, a bulb went off in her face. She blinked, momentarily blinded.

'And one more of you on your own. If you could move out of the way, please, Mother.'

'Erm, who are you?' Roisin asked once her vision was restored.

The clean-cut, eager beaver jumping about with a camera in front of her flashed a card at her. 'Press.'

'You came!' Maureen clapped her hands. 'Grand.'

Roisin thought she should have known this was down to Mammy. Still, and all free publicity for the studio had to be good.

'I'm Ger Collins,' the man elaborated. 'Reporter on the beat for Howth Happenings.'

A murmuring whipped through the party-goers, and there was much hair fluffing and striking of poses because Howth Happenings was a monthly magazine with a who's who in Howth's social page.

How had Mammy swung this? Roisin wondered because the magazine was also a glossy supplement choc full of advertising for the various Howth businesses. Her start-up budget hadn't stretched to taking an advertisement out for the studio, but she'd planned to once they were turning a profit. This, however, was a freebie, which was even better. There weren't many people in this world for whom Maureen O'Mara would move out of the way. Not if she could help it, especially if a camera was involved. However, meek as a lamb, she did just that and let Ger Collins take a snap of Roisin.

'I hoped to get here earlier but couldn't find a park,' he explained once he had his shot. Then, turning to face the audience who'd gathered for Roisin's speech, said, 'So don't mind me, everybody carry on as you were. I'll wander about, take a few snaps, and jot down names.

Worried that Mammy might take it upon herself to order the rest of the family up to stand alongside her for a photo, which, from past experience, could take some time to arrange everyone to her satisfaction, Roisin decided to crack on with her speech. She took a deep breath, hoping it would steady her voice.

'Welcome to the Bendy Yoga Studio, everyone.'

Someone near the door shouted, 'Speak up there, young lady, I've not got my hearing aids in.'

Roisin's insides squirmed, and she was momentarily thrown. Her mam slipped an arm around her waist, and she reminded herself this was her special day and she had something she wanted to say. She took another deep breath and, this time, all but shouted, 'I want to thank everyone who's come along this afternoon to celebrate what is the culmination of a dream come true for me. Here at the Bendy Yoga Studio, I wanted to create a space where everybody would feel welcome to come whether or not they've experienced the sense of well-being Yoga can bring into your life. I've worked hard to create classes catering for every age and ability, and I hope to see you at one of those.' Roisin paused, and a round of applause went up, although she thought whoever let rip with the piercing whistle was taking things a tad too far.

'I also wanted to take a moment to thank my mam, Maureen O'Mara, whom most of you know, for helping me make this studio happen. Thank you too, Shay, for being by my side through all the ups and downs to get to this point and Noah for putting up with my mind being elsewhere this last while.' Was she in danger of sounding like she was giving her acceptance speech at the Oscars? Time for a change of tact, 'Erm, there's something to be said for family, and I'm so lucky to have the support mine gives me. Ash, Moira, Tom, Quinn, Kiera, Aoife and Connor, Donal, Jodie and Philip,' should she include Pat and Cindy? Yes, she'd better because Donal was after videoing her, and she'd mentioned the twins and Kiera, who hadn't done anything either. 'And Patrick and Cindy, who can't be here with us today. 'Thank you for being my rocks. I love you all. Namaste.' She steepled her hands in prayer fashion and dipped her head.

'Sure, I didn't know your Rosi spoke another language, Maureen,' Bold Brenda piped up.

Another round of applause rippled around the room, and Roisin, enjoying the feeling of elation of having overcome her nerves to give her speech, which had been well received, became aware of an insistent mobile phone ringing nearby.

She'd one eye on Noah, who was piling the remaining cakes and slices on his plate and was about to tell him to leave some for others. Donal, meanwhile, had set aside the video recorder and was taking his place in front of the microphone as the rest of The Gamblers took up their positions. The phone was still ringing.

'Oh, it's my mobile phone,' Maureen announced, patting herself down.

Precisely one minute, thirty seconds later, though, instead of Donal taking the microphone, Maureen grabbed it, and her voice boomed around the studio.

'Patrick's after giving birth!'

Chapter Twenty-one

♥

Tiny beads of water clung to the little red fox's fur this morning, thanks to the steady drizzle. It was forecast to get heavier as the day went on.

This morning, the damp was the sort that would seep into your bones, Polly thought, wrapping her cardigan tightly about her. Wet weather always made the arthritis worse, which, given Ireland was her home, meant there wasn't much of a reprieve from her aches and pains these days. Right now, though, she'd forgotten about her ailments as she watched the fox snaffle his fat piece of white pudding served as a starter. It was always gratifying to see food being enjoyed, and it was apparent her new friend had missed her over the weekend, given he'd been there waiting for her as soon as she opened the door this morning.

Before going home on Friday, Polly had left a note for Mrs Baicu, who did the breakfast shift of a weekend, asking her to scrape any of the guest's leftovers into the container she'd left out for her on the bench. Now, Polly and Mrs Baicu's paths didn't often cross, which was a blessing given they viewed one another as the competition, so what the cook who hailed from Romania would make of Polly's request was anyone's guess. As for Polly, well, she hadn't so much as batted an eye as she'd further scribbled out a convoluted explanation as to how her grandson, the one whose mam and dad had acreage and a few farm animals in Wicklow (as though Mrs Baicu was in the know when it came to Polly's family) was after getting a pet pig and had asked for scraps. She'd only stopped short of giving the fabricated pet pig a name. Padraig had a grand ring to it, and she stashed it away as a suggestion for any future grandsons. Sure, it was a good, strong Irish name. They could do with a Padraig in the family.

Mrs Baicu had obliged, and it had been gratifying to open the fridge this morning and see the container filled with tasty titbits for her new foxy friend. Polly also found it gratifying that the little fox's ribs were no longer protruding, nor was his limp so pronounced. She'd always put plenty of store by the power of good food, and if that wasn't proof, then she didn't know what was.

She thought it was a satisfying arrangement they'd come to, herself and the fox, ensuring she stayed dry under the eaves. He ate, and she chatted. Who'd have thought a fox, of all things, would prove to be an ideal sounding board? And she'd lots to be telling him this morning after the weekend's shenanigans.

The thing Polly liked most about their understanding was he never answered back, unlike her children. Finola's smug face flittered forth as she recalled their conversation last night with a spark of irritation. Her middle daughter had telephoned on the dot of seven for their scheduled weekly half-hour catch-up. Her children were all very busy people, Finola included, and Polly happened to know that her daughter had pencilled her Sunday night phone call home in her diary. She'd seen the entry inadvertently once herself, under the heading: Telephone Mam and Dad. A half-hour window of time had been blocked out. It had made her feel like they were a chore to be ticked off Finola's 'to-do' list.

To be fair, it wasn't easy these days with it being the norm for both couples to work full time when you'd children to take care of as well. Finola would say goodbye to her at seven-thirty, never a minute later because she'd the ironing for the week ahead to tackle. At the same time, her husband would herd the children upstairs for their bath. Polly had once made the mistake of suggesting that if Finola and her husband had bought a smaller house in a less pricey suburb and hadn't upgraded their cars every other year, Finola wouldn't have had to work full time. It had turned out Finola had a mouth to match her mam's upon hearing that sentiment, and Polly had never voiced it again. Still and all, she stood by what she said, unable to fathom when things like where you lived, what you drove and where your children went to school had begun to matter so much. You thought you were well off in her day if you ate three meals daily.

During last night's conversation, Polly had told Finola about the party she'd gone to with Bronagh to celebrate the opening of Roisin's yoga studio in Howth. She'd excitedly relayed having her photo taken for Howth Happenings. Then there was the surprise baby announcement. She'd left out the part about how she and Bronagh had fancied themselves to be Celine Dion and Enya singing their hearts out on the DART ride back to the city, having well and truly celebrated the good news. Nor had she told Finola how she'd been green when she woke up on Sunday morning, and John Joseph had brought her tea and toast in bed when there'd been no sign of life by ten am.

No, she'd decided, there wasn't any need for her daughter to know the finer points, but then, she'd made the mistake of telling Finola she'd agree to try out next Saturday's class for seniors. Finola had only stopped laughing long enough to shout up the stairs to her husband that her mam was only after signing up for a yoga class, and could you picture her doing the downward dog? Polly had testily retorted that she'd not be sticking her arse up in the air for anybody, thanks very much and that Roisin had assured her she only needed to do what she was comfortable with. The conversation had further deteriorated when to get her daughter off the subject of downward dogs, she'd mentioned she'd made her peace with the fox that raided the bin in the courtyard of O'Mara's.

Polly relayed how she'd tossed the fox a few scraps because the creature looked terribly thin and had a limp. She knew she'd made a mistake mentioning this, hearing Finola give that sharp intake of breath that signalled she was about to deliver a dressing down in the voice usually reserved for the Courtroom. Polly held the phone away from her ear, pulling faces as her daughter prattled on about how feeding a wild animal would do it more harm than good because it would stop foraging for food and become reliant on her.

'Sure, was it better she let the poor thing starve then was it?' Polly had pounced back, but it was seven-thirty by then, and Finola was already saying goodbye.

Polly loved her children, Finola included, but she could be a terrible know-it-all at times.

The little fox's ears twitched as she packed her daughter away until next Sunday evening and informed him, 'I've a nice piece of brack for your afters this morning. It was going mouldy because I'm not a fan of the stuff. I only bake it for John Joseph, and he's after announcing he's on a health kick. He's a bowls tournament coming up. I don't mind telling you, there's always a fecking tournament coming up with that bowls he's so fond of. The man lives and breathes it, so he does. I'm a bowls widow,' she added theatrically. 'And I can't stand to see food go to waste, not after having watched my mam make a cheap cut of meat stretch from stew to soup to feed us when the money was tight.' Polly thought about the shine her husband had on yesterday afternoon when he'd come home looking for his dinner. 'Mind this health kick of John Joseph's is very selective because he's still managing to squeeze in a pint or two after he's finished practising for the tournament.' Polly shook her head. 'That man of mine can be a prize eejit at times.' But her tone had a fondness that suggested she wouldn't have it any other way.

The fox was making short work of the sausage now. 'Oh, and I've good news. Happy news. Patrick's wife Cindy over there in Los Angeles is after giving birth to a baby girl on Saturday. She was nearly nine pounds, and Maureen says most of that was probably in the head because the O'Mara babbies all have the pumpkin-headed gene. It's hard to believe all the O'Mara children are parents themselves now. It doesn't seem five minutes ago, Patrick was flying about the place dressed as Superman, or was it Spiderman? It could have been both, now I think about it.' She smiled at the memory. 'He'd come down to the kitchen and insist that everybody knew superheroes needed rasher sandwiches to give them their superhero powers. I never sent him away empty-handed.' A frown puckered her forehead. 'It's a blessing he grew out of that next phase of his when he took to doing the rebel yell and wearing the ripped singlets, even in the winter-like, and those leather trousers of his.' Polly shuddered.

'He drove his poor mammy mad with worry over his personal hygiene because he couldn't get the fecking trousers off once he'd got them on. In the end, Maureen had to take a pair of scissors to them. They were after cutting his circulation off. When you think about it, it's a miracle Patrick's managed to father a child given what he put his bits and bobs through.' Polly made a tutting sound, and then her eyes flitted skyward.

'Maureen and Donal were after flying out last night to Los Angeles to see the babby. Cindy, that's Patrick's wife, is American, and she's an actress. Maureen's terribly worried she'll have named the poor wee babby girl something like Moonbeam Aurora before they arrive. You know yourself what those Hollywood types are like when it comes to naming their children. Anyway, a new babby in the family is lovely news, alright.'

She moved away from the door and went to fetch the brack. 'Here we go, fella.' His eyes fixed on hers momentarily, and Polly fancied she saw a flicker of gratitude. 'You're welcome, so you are.'

Chapter Twenty-two

♥

'Right, you are to be a good boy, do you understand me? It's very kind of your Aunty Rosemary to agree to watch you while I'm busy in the studio,' Roisin said to Pooh as they reached the laneway leading to her studio. Her studio! A pop of excitement exploded in Roisin's chest. Today, she was officially in business, and she patted about the pocket of her pink jacket for the keys with her spare hand, reassuring herself they were still there. Pooh, however, had stopped trotting alongside her and was doing his best statue imper-sonation as he gave a low growl. Roisin frowned. She did not need a prima-donna poodle, not today of all days.

'Now you can cut that out. You get on very well with Rosemary, so you do.' She huffed and tugged his leash. This was what you got for counting your chickens before they hatched or whatever the saying was. Roisin had kept a wary distance and a tight hold of Pooh as she waved Noah in through the school gates this morning. Watching her son disappear into the care of Mrs Dunlop for the day, she'd been feeling quietly confident that perhaps having Pooh to stay with them for the week Mammy and Donal were in Los Angeles wouldn't be so bad after all.

Rosemary had initially volunteered her dog-care services, having had Pooh stay with her once before. Still, Noah had begged, pleaded, and cajoled until Roisin caved and told Mammy the poodle would be welcome at their house. Shay hadn't minded in the least, but Roisin suspected that was because he was still doing his utmost to ingratiate himself where Mammy was concerned. Upon hearing this, Moira said he was in danger of becoming a fecky brown noser. She also suspected she would regret giving in to Noah because it would be her looking after him, and Pooh was a high-maintenance dog.

'Come on with you now,' Roisin ordered, and Pooh reluctantly slunk after her over the slick cobbles to his home for the next few hours. Carrick's the Cobblers, where he promptly cocked his leg outside the door in protest. A light glowed invitingly through the shop window, and pushing the door open, Roisin stepped into the leathery-smelling interior. 'Morning Cathal.' She only just stopped herself from tacking on Carrick the Cobbler to the greeting. 'Come on, Pooh, Aunty Rosemary's looking forward to seeing you. You'll have a lovely time,' she muttered through gritted teeth.

Pooh sat down on his haunches in the doorway and glared at her. Jaysus wept. This was worse than taking a reluctant toddler along to a playgroup; she thought only she'd not feel an ounce of guilt dropping and running today.

'Good morning, Roisin. Today's the day then.' Cathal looked up from his inspection of a boat shoe's sole from behind the counter. 'Would you mind closing that door behind you? You're letting all the cold air in.'

'I would if I could, Cathal, but Pooh's refusing to budge. I'm afraid he's not in good form. He doesn't like change.'

'Oh, don't be worrying about that, Roisin.' Rosemary sprang up from behind the counter as she was apt to do.

It was a mystery as to what she found to do down there, Roisin thought, giving the lead another tug to no avail. Pooh was doing a sit-in protest.

'I've got just the ticket,' Rosemary said. 'Wait there a minute.' She paused her hand on the door leading through to the workroom. 'Have you heard from your Mammy and Donal?'

'Not yet, Rosemary. I expect we will this evening sometime. We're all eager for news about our little niece and how Cindy's getting on.'

'Your mammy was after telling me the birth was very traumatic for Patrick, too.'

'Patrick finds a runny nose traumatic,' Roisin mumbled.

'What was that?'

'Nothing, Rosemary.'

'Well, be sure and let me know when you hear.'

'I will.'

Roisin and Pooh eyeballed one another while waiting to see what trick Rosemary had up her sleeve. They didn't have to wait long because music suddenly blared from the workroom. Pooh's ears pricked while Roisin winced. She recognised the tune. Was it Glen Campbell? Rhinestone Cowboy, perhaps? Yes, she concluded, it was as Rosemary came thunking out in time to get her groove on, on the shop floor along to the chorus. Dear God, was the woman pretending she'd reins in her hand as she bobbed up and down? Pooh yipped and yapped, tugging free of the lead, and trotting off toward Rosemary with a wag in his stumpy, curly-haired tail. He broke out some pretty groovy paw work to rival the woman who thought she was the Rhinestone Cowgirl.

'Works a treat every time, Roisin,' Rosemary said over the music. 'He loves his country music, don't you, Pooh?'

Roisin shook her head. She'd seen it all now and, not wanting to hang about any longer, called out, 'Thanks!' and pulled the door behind her. Seconds later, she tried to steady her hand to fit the key in the lock next door. It was anticipation over this morning's ten am class. Her very first class was a fully booked session aimed at new mothers. Babies were welcome because she didn't want any barriers to coming along, like having to find a babysitter for an hour. She knew how reluctant she'd have been to leave Noah when he was tiny with anyone who wasn't family. She also knew how much she'd have loved to have been able to attend something like the classes The Bendy Yoga Studio was offering without feeling uncomfortable if she needed to leave her mat to tend to her baby.

Aisling was coming along with Moira and the twins, but Kiera would spend the morning with her other nana. They'd go for a coffee afterwards because Roisin's next class wasn't until midday. She appreciated her sisters driving to Howth to support her because their familiar faces would see off the rest of her nerves.

An envelope had been slid under the door, she noted. Stooping to pick it up and flipping it over, she saw the official council address. Well, that could wait. Taking the stairs two at a time, Roisin opened the door to the studio, eagerly flicking the light switch. She had a class to be getting ready for!

No evidence remained of Saturday's shin-dig thanks to her and Shay getting stuck in with a couple of bin bags, a damp cloth, hoover and having given the studio a good airing out. Mammy and Donal had kept an eye on Noah while they packed for their drop-everything trip to LA. The party had gone over well, Bold Brenda and her carry-on being the only exception. She was still thinking of slapping her with a studio ban even if Mammy had said that went against her inclusivity philosophy.

The place was comfortably warm, which meant the timer was working for the heating, and she slipped out of her jacket, hanging it on the back of a chair in the kitchen. The first batch of Bendy Yoga Ladies jackets was due for delivery this week, Mammy had informed her as she'd driven her and Donal to the airport in their car. A few were already earmarked for those who'd opted for a year's subscription. Roisin had tuned her out when she got to not forgetting to water her pot plants, to feed the Christmas Cakes she had on the go with a splash of whiskey each day, and that Pooh was partial to a nice bit of steak on Fridays. She hoped the pavement sign would arrive today because she was worried about how those who hadn't come to the party or visited Carrick's the Cobbler's shop in the past would find them. The lane was blink and you'd miss it if you didn't know it was there. There was no point worrying about that now, though, and she laid the mats out, placing a block and strap beside each of them. She switched the diffuser on, enjoying its lemony scent and checked that all she had to do was press play on the Spiritual Flow CD. Yes, she thought, running through the notes she'd made for the class, she was good to go.

Roisin checked her watch; there were still twenty minutes until class. Aisling and Moira should be here any minute. They'd promised to arrive ten or so minutes early for moral support. Roisin realised that the studio was strangely silent without Mammy breathing down her neck. They'd been joined at the hip virtually for weeks, and even though it was a relief to have some space from her helpfulness, it was odd. 'Make the most of it, Roisin,' she said out loud, 'She'll be back before you know it.'

The news of a new baby girl in the family had been met with great excitement on Saturday afternoon, and there'd been much wetting of the baby's head. They'd all taken turns, party guests included, to hop on Mam's mobile and congratulate their brother and sister-in-law, who'd sounded shell-shocked, to say the least. Mind you, so would she if a line of strangers had got on the phone to congratulate her minutes after she'd given birth to Noah. She couldn't wait to see the first photos of the little family, which Mammy was no doubt busy snapping this very minute. Would her niece take after Cindy or Patrick, or would she be a mix of them both? One thing was guaranteed. She'd have good teeth!

Cindy would find having her mammy-in-law staying a mixed blessing, Roisin suspected. On the plus side, the new mother wouldn't have to lift a finger about the place for her mammy-in-law's stay. Without worrying about what was for dinner or attempting to tidy up the place, she could concentrate on nothing but herself, Patrick and the baby. This would come at a cost, though, because in return, she'd have to listen to lots and lots of helpful Mammy tips.

Roisin and her sisters had done their best by their sister-in-law by suggesting that Mammy and Donal might like to book a hotel for their Los Angeles stay to give Patrick and Cindy a chance to settle into the business of being parents. Cindy's folks and her sister had opted to come a fortnight after Maureen and Donal had been and gone to stagger out being of use to their daughter. But no, Mammy had been adamant a hotel wouldn't work, not with her needing to be on hand twenty-four/seven.

What would her niece be called? Roisin wondered, then remembering the envelope she'd dropped on the table in the kitchen, she fetched it, ripping it open.

The paper she held in her hand was crisp, white and official. Her eyes scanned through the paragraph, and then she re-read it slower this time because surely this was a joke? But no, the message was clear, laid out in plain black typeface.

Roisin heard the door below bang shut, followed by echoing voices in the stairwell. It was followed by her sisters bickering as they lugged the baby carriers up the stairs. Under normal circumstances, she'd hope they hadn't had to park too far away. Still, these were anything but because right now, she felt as if the letter could combust at any second into flames.

'Rosi! Jaysus wept the traffic was terrible this morning. You'd better appreciate us being here. I'm thinking it will be your treat for coffee and cake later. And you know yourself you take your life in your hands when you get in the car with Moira,' Aisling's voice trailed off, catching sight of her.

Moira banging on about being a perfectly good driver was bringing up the rear.

'Rosi?' Aisling queried setting a sleeping Aoife down.

Moira pushed past her older sister, still holding on to Connor's carrier. 'What's wrong? You've not heard from Mam, have you? Is the baby alright?' Twenty questions were fired off.

'No, I've not heard from Mam. I'm sure everything's fine over there.' Roisin rattled the piece of paper. 'It's this.'

Aisling strode over, snatching the paper off her sister to run a hasty eye over the text.

'Read it out loud,' Moira demanded.

'I don't have to. The gist is that Rosi should have applied to the District Court for a public dance and music licence, given she was hosting an event.'

Moira snorted, and Connor stared up at her uncertainly. 'But that's ridiculous. It was a private party.'

Aisling shrugged. 'Not exactly. It was promotional if you wanted to get picky.'

'It was Mammy's big idea to hold a party,' Roisin's voice wobbled. 'Smart marketing.'

'It's hardly Mammy's fault that some eejit pencil pusher has decided to make an example of you.'

'Is Rosi facing jail time?' Moira's brown eyes were enormous.

'Feck off Moira,' Roisin snapped.

'Don't be stupid, Moira. A fine, maybe, although this is more of a letter than an infringement notice. But then, I'm not a lawyer.'

'I'll come and visit you and sneak you in a phone, Rosi,' Moira said generously.

'Shut up, Moira. You're not helping.' Aisling frowned and flapped the paper. 'Don't you think it's a little strange that this has arrived first thing Monday morning and the party was only held on Saturday? Was it hand delivered or something?'

'It was on the doormat when I arrived,' Roisin supplied. 'Ash, they can't shut me down for this, can they?'

'Whoa, slow down, Rosi. You're supposed to be the calm yoga teacher here. Like I said, it's a letter, nothing official, but if it goes further, I'd say you'll get some sort of fine and a slap on the hand.'

'You also said you're not a lawyer,' Roisin's voice trembled.

'Rosi, you've a class to teach in five minutes. Pull yourself together, do your special childbirth breathing or something.' Aisling picked up the discarded envelope and stuffed the notice inside it. Then, picking up Aoife, she carried her through to the kitchen. Moira followed after her.

Aisling was right, Roisin thought. She needed to get herself in the right head space. Accordingly, she pursed her lips in an O shape. She exhaled slowly, inhaling for a shorter time before exhaling again. What Aisling had just said about the letter arriving so promptly being strange was swirling about her head. Something didn't make sense.

But as the door banged below, she put it out of her mind. She had a class to teach.

Chapter
Twenty-three

'Two pink lady jackets, gone,' Moira stated. 'Do I need to tick them off some sort of Inventory list, and do I get a commission for selling the annual subscriptions?'

'Feck off, Moira,' Roisin replied. The studio was still warm with the recent bodies who'd filled it.

'Charming. Well, I expect you to spring for a coffee and a slice of Millionaire's shortbread down at that Piratey café on the main street there at the very least.'

That she could do, given her next class wasn't until after lunchtime, Roisin thought with a grin. Eventually, she hoped to be holding back-to-back classes, but that would be a slow build, and she was off to a great start with the bookings she'd had as it was. She rolled up the last straps, straightened a couple of mats, and was ready for the next class. She'd put aside the ridiculous letter now and was on a natural high. Yoga always left her with a sense of well-being and coupled with the feedback after class from mam's who'd said they'd definitely be back and how much they'd enjoyed the session, she was floating.

Incorporating a few stretches for those babies wide awake toward the end of the class was also fun. Most gratifying of all, though, had been hearing a woman with curls escaping her ponytail tentatively inviting the others back to her place for a cup of tea. Like herself, she was new to the area she'd explained, and Roisin had smiled as her address was handed out because this was precisely what she'd hoped for. To bring people together.

There'd only been two no-shows on the mat, which was perfectly understandable given that you were dealing with babies. Nobody had minded in the least when a woman called Gemma had to disappear mid-way through the class to sit in the kitchen to feed her little boy, or when another wee one in the sweetest tiny hedgehog print stretch-n-grow began to howl and as for the unmistakable smell of filled nappy wafting through as they enjoyed a well-earned Savasana at the end of the session, nobody was in the least bit phased. It was an aroma they were all well used to. Her students booked in next might not be, though, Roisin thought, wondering whether she should open the window or whether that would cool the studio down too much. In the end, she dug out the bottle of Arpège air freshener Mammy had left under the kitchen sink and waved it around the place. Moira's protests about feeling like Mammy was hiding in the studio were ignored.

Roisin had kept the routine for her first class gentle. She'd focussed on Bridge poses, Downward facing Dogs, Cats and Cows, pausing in the arching of her back to glare at Moira, who was mumbling they'd be doing a fecking pig rolling in the mud next. She'd have to have a word with Aisling about investing in a decent sports bra if she planned on coming to another class. It had been touch and go as to whether there would be fallout during the Downward Dogs and Forward Bends.

'Come on then, Rosi. I'm starving, and these two will be too. I'll feed them at the café,' Aisling, already in her pink lady jacket, said as she hefted the baby carrier up.

'I'll take Connor,' Roisin volunteered once she'd pulled her jacket on. She crouched down to tuck the blanket around her nephew and pull his hat up, which had slipped over one eye. She stroked his cheek gently. 'How's my boy?' She got a gummy smile by way of return with no sign of the teeth Aisling said had been plaguing him.

'Do you think we look like eejits in our jackets?' Moira asked, zipping hers up against the cold and eyeing her sisters.

'Probably,' Aisling said, heading for the door, 'But sure, it's not as if we're likely to see anyone we know in Howth, and Mammy can't say we're not doing our bit. You know what she's like. The woman has eyes and ears everywhere. If we don't wear them, one of her informers is bound to report us.'

'It's alright for you two. I'm after living here now. I nearly died when Mammy presented me with mine, but it's sort of growing on me, and fair play to her, they're proving popular. Women want to be part of the Bendy Yoga Ladies group.'

'It's about belonging, isn't it. I mean, those two mammies couldn't wait to put their free jackets on after class,' Moira said, and her sisters gave one another a surprised glance because it was a profound comment for Moira.

'I suppose it is,' Roisin said.

'And, it's very warm. Surprisingly so,' Aisling said. 'The colour's not so bad either.'

'We're pretty in pink.' Moira flicked her hair out of the collar.

'Smart marketing is what it is,' Roisin said knowingly.

The sisters chattered down the stairs and out into the laneway. Roisin passed Connor to Moira so she could lock up. Then, linking their spare arms, they made their way to the piratey café, turning heads all the way.

The café was a little quieter, being a Monday, and they'd no bother commandeering a table down the back. 'I like a little bit of privacy when I'm feeding the babies,' Aisling said, unfastening Aoife, who had her fist in her mouth from her carrier. She shouted after Roisin, 'I'll have a large scone, Rosi, with jam and cream, please. Oh, and a herbal tea, I can't have caffeine, not when I'm breastfeeding.'

The whole café knew her sister was breastfeeding now, Roisin thought. So much for discretion. Ah, well, what did it matter? Moira, true to her word, went for the Millionaire's shortbread while Roisin decided to push the boat out with another cream slice. She thought, eat your heart out, Ciara, with a 'C' because I won't be buying you one. She'd no sooner paid when the door jingled open, and she heard her name called. With their order number in her hand, Roisin saw Becca beaming at her.

'What great timing! You can join us. I'm here celebrating a successful class with Aisling, Moira and the twins. My first.'

Becca waved at the sisters, who had met her on Saturday afternoon. 'The first of many, I'm sure. It went well then?'

'Great, thanks. Really great.'

'Oh, I am pleased for you, Rosi, and I'd love to join you and your sisters, but I can't. We're short-staffed thanks to a flu bug doing the rounds. I've only ducked out to get a sandwich and coffee to takeaway.'

'That's a shame.'

'Another time. And thanks so much for Saturday, by the way. Mam, Lottie and I had a brilliant time. It was so exciting when your mam announced you'd a new baby girl in the family.'

'It's brilliant news,' Roisin smiled.

'And then when the band began playing, and Brenda started with the leg kicks, I thought I would have an accident. I was laughing that hard.'

'Don't,' Roisin held her hand up to stop Becca from going down that track, but she was grinning. 'And we'll work on that pelvic floor when you come to a session.'

'What pelvic floor? It's been non-existent since Lottie.' Becca ploughed on before Roisin could comment. 'I wish you'd taken me up on my offer to help you with the clean-up on Sunday. Was it awful?'

'No. Sure, Shay and I made light work of it, but I did appreciate the offer.'

The piratey man was looking at Becca expectantly, and she placed her order and then stood to one side to wait for her coffee with Roisin.

'So has your mam and — '

'Donal.'

'Donal, sorry, I can't help but think of him as Kenny. Have they flown out to see the new baby?'

'They have. I've the use of Mammy and Donal's car, so I took them to the airport myself yesterday.' Roisin smiled. 'We're all waiting with bated breath to hear what Patrick and Cindy decide to call their little girl and to see some photographs, of course.'

'Of course.' Becca looked across the tables to where Aisling, Moira and the twins were.

'They've just attended their first yoga class.'

'Your sisters?'

'Sort of. They've had private sessions with me before, but no, I meant the twins.'

'They're absolutely adorable, and Aisling seems to manage to have two babies so well. I struggled with just the one!'

'She's had her ups and downs like we all do.'

'I'll duck over and say a quick hello.'

Roisin navigated after her.

'Hello there, I'm Becca. We met on Saturday.'

'Hi, Becca.' Aisling looked up from feeding Aoife.

'Lottie's Mam. Kiera thought she was great.' Moira grinned up at her waggling her fingers to entertain Connor while he waited his turn.

Becca smiled. 'I hope she wasn't too bossy. She's going through a phase.'

'It would take a strong woman to boss Kiera about, I don't mind telling you. She takes after her nana.'

They all laughed.

'Did Rosi tell you about the letter she's after getting?' Aisling asked, her expression sobering.

Becca looked at Roisin questioningly. 'No?'

'I forgot, believe it or not. I've been buzzing ever since the class finished.' She patted her pocket and then remembered it was back at the studio. 'I don't have it on me, but it was on official Council letterhead stating I should have applied to the District Court for a public dancing and music licence to hold the party at the studio.'

'Seriously?'

Roisin nodded, feeling her high beginning to evaporate at the thought of the fine likely heading her way. Not to mention the black mark against the studio's name with the official powers that be.

Aisling piped up again. 'It's strange how quickly it arrived, don't you think? The party was Saturday afternoon, and the letter was there waiting on the doormat Monday morning. Hand-delivered no less.'

'I wouldn't have thought the council was open on a Sunday or their mail was delivered personally.' Moira frowned and then shrugged. 'Then again, it is Howth. They probably do things a little differently.'

'I wouldn't have thought so, and it is odd,' Becca said, her brows furrowing. 'Was there a name on this letter?'

Roisin closed her eyes momentarily, trying to visualise the signature at the bottom. 'I think it was signed off by a T Buckley.'

Becca shook her head slowly. 'Oh, that's low.'

'What is?' All three women chimed, eyes trained on Becca.

'T Backley, or Terence Backley, is Philomena's husband. Don't you think that's too much of a coincidence?'

'One white coffee to go,' the young girl making the hot drinks called out.

'That's me. I've left the practice nurse manning reception, so I've got to run, but I'll call you tonight, Rosie?'

'I'd appreciate that, Becca, thanks.' Roisin watched her take a wide berth around the piratey man making his way toward them with his tray of sweet treats and hot drinks. Her mind was whirring, trying to understand what she'd just heard.

'Who's Philomena?' Moira demanded.

'Yeah, who's Philomena?' Aisling echoed.

Roisin waited until their order had been laid out before replying. 'Philomena is head of the Parents' Association at Noah's school, and it's her cockapoo that Pooh tried to get a leg over on Noah's first day.'

'So we think this Philomena is targeting you and the studio because Mammy's randy poodle tried to get friendly with her cockapoo?' Moira shook her head. 'That's mad.'

'I know,' Roisin said. 'Then there's the game.'

'What game?' The sisters were a double act.

Roisin explained how Noah had instigated a new version of an old favourite. Tag. 'It's not funny, Moira,' she said when finished.

'It's a vendetta,' Aisling breathed, eyes wide.

'We're in Howth, Ash, not Corsica.' However, if Philomena was behind the letter, then what her sister had said was true enough; it was a vendetta, albeit a ridiculous one.

'Do you think this Philomena could get the studio shut down if she set her mind to it?' Moira voiced what was worrying Roisin because that was not a ridiculous thought.

'I don't know Moira. I just don't know.'

'Let her try,' Aisling said.

'Yeah.' Moira pulled herself up to her grand height of five foot nothing. 'Nobody puts the O'Mara sisters in the corner.'

'You so stole that from Dirty Dancing,' Roisin and Aisling said.

Chapter

Twenty-four

♥

Roisin swallowed the last mouthful of her slice and was licking the cream off her fingers when her phone shrilled from her pocket. She dug it out, glanced at the screen and then from one to the other of her sisters. 'It's Mammy. Don't be telling her about the letter. I don't want her worrying.'

'I won't say a word,' Aisling said.

'She won't hear so much as a peep out of me,' Moira said.

Roisin was unsure whether they could be trusted, but as they jostled in next to her for a three-way conversation, she answered, eager for news of their baby niece.

'Hello, Mammy!'

A woman and her friend were chatting at a table next to them.

'Would you mind using your inside voices, please, our Mammy's after ringing us from Los Angeles,' Aisling called across to them.

Roisin knew exactly where she'd got that from, having heard Mammy telling Noah to use his inside voice more than once. The indignation on the women's faces would have been comical if she wasn't mortified. Aisling had better watch it because she was in danger of becoming a coppery-haired version of Mammy.

'Is that you, Roisin, Aisling and Moira?'

Mammy was definitely not using her inside voice.

'No, Mammy, it's your other three daughters, Drizella, Anastasia and me, of course, Cinderella.' Moira earned herself a jab in the ribs from Roisin. 'Ow!'

'I'm ringing you from Los Angeles on my mobile phone. I don't have time for the smart-arse remarks, Moira.'

'We're well aware you're in LA. I dropped you at the airport, remember?' Roisin pulled a face.

'Of course, I remember. There's nothing wrong with my memory, Roisin.'

True enough, it was like an elephant's.

'What time is it there, Mammy?' Aisling asked.

'It's just gone eight o'clock in the morning. I'm not long after having breakfast. If you can call it that. It was something you'd hang from a tree for the birds to peck at. It was full of little black seeds, and they're terrible for getting stuck in your teeth. Donal and I will head out later and get some proper food in. It's nourishment Cindy needs, given she's feeding the baby herself, not seeds.'

'They were good enough for me the other day when you wouldn't let me have the cream slice, Mammy.' Roisin felt a little put-out.

'That was smart marketing, Roisin. You've got to think about branding now you're in business, and cream slices don't go hand in hand with yoga, do they?'

She'd heard it all before, Roisin thought.

Meanwhile, Aisling was busy working out the time difference, announcing that Mammy was a day behind them over there in Los Angeles.

True to form, Moira got straight to the point of the call and asked, 'How's Cindy and the baby getting on?'

'Cindy's marvellous. Glowing she is. You want to see the hair on her. It's the shampoo adverts she wants to put herself forward for while the hormones are on her side, not the personal care. I said I'd mind the baby for her if she wanted to nip out for a quick shoot like because, you know yourselves, the lovely hair doesn't last. It will be all stringy and ratty before she knows it. I have to say, though, she's taken to motherhood like a duck to water. The babby's a wee dote, she's feeding ever so well, and she's the look of Patrick about her. She's definitely an O'Mara that wan.'

'Glad to hear it,' Moira muttered.

'Well, we'll think she's beautiful even if she does take after Pat,' Aisling said, making her sisters snigger.

Maureen sailed on obliviously. 'Actually, girls, it's Patrick I'm worried about. He doesn't cope well without his full eight hours of sleep a night, and like I was just after saying, he's not eating properly. There's nothing but seeds in the house.'

This time, all three sisters rolled their eyes.

'Has our niece a name yet? Or will she remain 'the babby' for the foreseeable future?' Aisling enquired, keen to get off the subject of Patrick.

'No, that's still being debated. But the hot favourite is Buttercup. I've told Patrick we won't be having a Buttercup O'Mara in the family, thank you very much, and that Bronwyn's got a lovely ring to it. He's to tell Cindy it would be a nod to her daughter's Irish heritage and that it's a grand compromise because it still begins with a 'B'.'

'I think you'll find Bronwyn's Welsh Mammy,' Roisin informed her.

'Anything's an improvement on Buttercup,' Moira muttered. 'Jaysus wept. Can you imagine the christening? What's her middle name going to be? Meadow?'

'You can keep that to yourself, Moira O'Mara. Don't be putting ideas in their head.'

Aisling moved the conversation along. 'And how was your flight, Mammy?'

'The service was a notch up from those Ryan Air flights to Santorini and home, I don't mind telling you. I was after ordering the chicken, and it came with a very nice tart for dessert. Donal enjoyed the beef, and we both had a glass of red to wash it down.'

'Well, the Ryan Air flights were no frills, Mammy,' Roisin reminded her.

'Would it have been that much of a bother for the flight attendants to offer us a cup of tea now? It's common manners is what it is, Roisin.'

There was no point arguing with her, Roisin thought.

'And Donal's got the swollen ankles. Terrible puffy they are.'

'Cankles.' Moira supplied.

'They're after giving me an idea.'

'Brace yourselves.'

'I heard that Moira.'

'Ignore her, Mammy,' Aisling said. 'What's your idea?'

'Mo-socks for the air travel.'

'Ah, no, Mammy.' A unanimous vote vetoed the idea.

But 'No' was a foreign word to Maureen. 'A woman was sitting beside me with a fine pair of snowy white socks on her feet. They were special ones, tight like to stop the swelling.

'I think you'll find a market for compression socks already exists, Mammy,' Aisling said.

'Ah, but I think there's a niche market for the Mo-sock. I'll look into it when I'm home. Did I tell you we were after getting a discounted rate on our taxi fare to Patrick and Cindy's apartment?'

'No Mammy.'

'Our driver, Rick, was his name. Well, his great-great-grandmother's cousin's sister hailed from Bally-something-or-other. She emigrated to America in the eighteen hundreds, but Rick takes his ties to the home country seriously. I told him if he comes to Ireland, he's to stay at O'Mara's, so keep your eyes peeled, Aisling. Look out for Rick, who drives a taxi in Los Angeles, and give him a discount. Quid-pro-quo.'

'Mammy, don't be saying things like quid-pro-quo,' Moira said. 'It's annoying.'

'Have you been taking lots of photos, Mammy?' Aisling asked.

'I've used a whole film already.'

'We can't wait to see them.'

Moira and Roisin agreed.

'Will you get Patrick to send one through on the internet. We're desperate for a look at Buttercup.'

'Her name is not Buttercup, Moira.'

'It's growing on me.'

'Don't be winding Mammy up.' Aisling elbowed her sister once more.

'And how was your first session, Rosi? I thought of you even though it's not until tomorrow here.'

Roisin decided there was no point in trying to make sense of that, telling her how well it had gone.

'And I'm after signing two mammies up for the year,' Moira butted in.

'It was the jackets that did it, Mammy,' Aisling said.

'See, Roisin, what I have been telling you?'

'Smart marketing Mammy.'

'Very good.'

'And Roisin's after getting a letter from the Council, Mammy all official like saying she needed special licences for the party,' Moira blurted.

Roisin stomped on her foot, mouthing, 'Thanks a million.'

Moira pulled a face back at her.

'What's this all about, Roisin?'

'It's a vendetta, Mammy,' Moira jumped in again, leaving Roisin with no choice but to fill her in on the letter and their suspicions. The driving force behind it was Philomena from the Parents Association.

'It doesn't pay to get on the wrong side of some people in a small place, Mammy,' Roisin said.

'No,' Maureen said darkly. 'It certainly doesn't, but it doesn't pay to get on the wrong side of an O'Mara either. I'll sort it when I'm home.'

Chapter Twenty-five

♥

Polly opened the door to the courtyard. The day was forecast to be crisp but clear, a welcome respite from all the rain they'd been having. 'It's only me,' she said to the fox, waiting close enough to the hole under the wall that he could dart back through if she made any sudden move. 'I've a nice piece of black pudding for you this morning. You'll want to eat that up because there's plenty of iron in it, and I brought you a slice of meatloaf. John Joseph and I had it for dinner last night. Very tasty it was too. It's the tomato sauce I put in that gives it extra flavour. But don't be telling anyone. That's our secret.' How she'd explain where the last slice of the meatloaf John Joseph had said would do him nicely for his lunch had gone, she didn't know!

Polly tossed the scraps into the middle of the courtyard and stayed where she was in the doorway. 'Come on with you now. You know I'm not going to hurt you.'

Keeping a wary eye on her, the fox slunk over and began to tuck in.

Stifling a yawn, Polly said, 'I couldn't sleep last night.' It wasn't that she was cold or too hot. It wasn't even because of John Joseph's sporadic snores that would make you jump as they let you know he was still breathing. She'd been lying on her back with her eyes open, staring at the distinctive shape of the seventies light fitting that they'd never bothered updating because she was stewing.

Finola had telephoned out of the blue after they'd finished their dinner wanting her stuffing recipe for the turkey because she'd be hosting Christmas this year.

'But we always have Christmas here. It's your home,' Polly had said. She was on the back foot because it wasn't Sunday and her daughter was phoning her. Now Finola was telling her, no less, not asking how she felt about it, that they'd be breaking with the tradition of a lifetime.

'Ah, Mam. I just think it's getting a bit much for you. Sure, enjoy putting your feet up for a day and being waited on.'

But Polly didn't want to put her feet up and be waited on. She wanted to be run off her feet in the kitchen, seeing to the potatoes, basting the turkey and slapping hands away from the trifle in the fridge.

Finola could be very assertive when she wanted to be and had already informed her brothers and sisters of the change in plan.

It made Polly fret she wasn't needed anymore. Sure, even John Joseph had made himself an omelette when she'd gone off to Roisin's party with Bronagh last Saturday. He hadn't starved without her.

So there she'd been wide awake and stewing over her matriarch's role being usurped by Finola when a rogue thought sneakily wormed its way into her head, and it refused to be quietened.

Was she lonely?

Polly pooh-poohed this as ridiculous because she was hardly alone. The snoring fella next to her was evidence of that. Then there were her children. Yes, they were busy living their lives, but they loved her; she knew that. She had her work at the guesthouse too, and... and...'

That was when she'd known sleep would elude her because, and what? Her confidante these days was the little red fox.

Perhaps what had her so out of sorts of late wasn't her aching hands and fear of being put on the scrap heap but that she was lonely. The idea made her feel strange. Was John Joseph right? Did she need a hobby? Something of her own.

As she brooded, it dawned on Polly she'd equated being busy with being needed. And, for as long as she could remember, she'd always been busy. Somewhere along the way, her friendships had fallen by the wayside, and her world had downsized to her family, work, and not much else. She'd forgotten how to stop and smell those roses, as the saying went.

Adaptability had never been a strength; but adapt she would have to do. She needed to learn to enjoy the changes getting older brought. Besides, hadn't Finola asked her for her stuffing recipe? As for John Joseph, his omelette had stuck to the frying pan! He was a long way from being self-sufficient. Her family still needed her, but in different ways.

Polly thought about Roisin's party last Saturday and how much she'd enjoyed Bronagh's company away from work. There'd been a whole studio full of women around their age. Perhaps they could extend an open invitation to lunch after the yoga class. It would be a good way to get to know new people. She'd felt a slow, burning excitement build.

John Joseph had his bowls, and it was high time she found something for her. He was right. Not that she'd be telling him that. She might not feel old, but she was getting older, a blessing plenty weren't afforded. She would embrace it, not rail at it.

'It's time I stepped outside my comfort zone,' she told Mr Fox. Polly could have sworn he dipped his head in a nod of agreement.

Chapter Twenty-six

♥

Roisin's welcoming smile was firmly in place even as she questioned the wisdom of offering men's only classes. Donal had put the idea in her head, and he wasn't even here! She'd been sold on creating a space aimed at the male, retired from work, but not life demographic of Howth. Somewhere, men felt comfortable and not outnumbered by the women. A space where they didn't have to feel self-conscious or silly. She had never considered creating a space for parading in your cycling shorts. The local bike shop must have had a run on the fecking things because she'd not been prepared to see so much Lycra filling her studio.

The bicycle shorts were all well and good for the cycling. Actually, no. Scratch that. Bicycle shorts were never a good idea, and certainly not for doing the Proud Warriors or Triangle poses. She wouldn't even think about the Downward Facing Dogs! Just don't look down, Roisin, she told herself, adding sternly, keep your eyes raised at all times and remember you're a professional. Dear God, was that a banana your man over there had down his pants? Her eyes were watering. Wait until Aisling and Moira heard about this. Becca, too, would find it hysterical. She'd have to have a quiet word in Mammy's ear when she got home because it wouldn't do for Donal to be wearing the Lycra when he attended next week. That would push her over the edge.

Banana man was taking things very seriously too. The class didn't start for another five minutes, but he was throwing himself into warm-up lunges that would make Mammy proud. Nobody loved a good lunge like Mammy.

To take her mind off the sights she knew once seen couldn't be unseen, Roisin mulled over the week. Her first five days in business had gone well despite the rocky Monday morning start, thanks to T Backley. Bookings were rolling in as word of mouth spread, and she'd seen more than a few Bendy Yoga Ladies pink jackets being flaunted about the village, too. Word was spreading because fellow mams were coming up to her to ask about the classes she offered when she saw Noah off to school each morning from a safe distance with Pooh. Most satisfying, though, was she'd managed everything independently because with Mammy in LA, she was her own boss, and she liked it. It would be hard to return to having her daily presence and input when she came home. As for that letter from Philomena's arsey husband in his official council capacity, she and Becca had concluded Philomena merely wanted to rattle her because nothing further had been forthcoming. What had motivated her was beyond Roisin, but she wouldn't stoop to her level, and she'd have to try and ensure Mammy didn't either when she got back. With this in mind, Roisin waved out upon seeing Philomena offloading her brood outside school each morning. She hadn't waved back.

Shay said the spiteful act might be down to something as plain and simple as jealousy. Roisin was new to the village and making a splash with her business, he'd said as they shared a bottle of red the other evening.

They were recovering from the drama that had unfolded before sitting down to dinner when she'd been stirring the curry, and Shay had been seeing to the rice. Noah had appeared in the kitchen announcing Mr Nibbles was missing, and he suspected Pooh might have something to do with it because he kept licking his chops. For once, it had transpired that the poodle was wrongly accused, because Mr Nibbles was found relaxing behind the toilet cistern.

Who knew? This had been Roisin's response to Shay's jealousy theory. It was hard to fathom how a silly incident with an over-excited poodle was behind the stupid letter. People could be peculiar, and that's all there was to it. She wasn't going to waste any more energy on it. Bigger things were going on, like the arrival of her beautiful new niece. Patrick had sent through several photos, and they were all smitten with the 'Babby,' Her brother and sister-in-law were still no closer to naming her. Although Buttercup was still in the running. Like she'd said to Shay the other night, she thought people could be peculiar.

Her faith in humanity was restored as a retiree who'd mercifully opted for baggy bottoms walked through the door, and she smiled in welcome. All the mats were occupied, which meant it was time for her to introduce herself and explain what to expect over the next hour.

Here goes, Roisin thought, taking a deep breath.

Chapter
Twenty-seven

♥

'It was very good of you to pick me up, Mrs Flaherty,' Bronagh said as they crossed the road from where Mrs Flaherty had nabbed a parking spot on Howth's busy main street. 'You're an excellent driver with all those forward and backward manoeuvres you were after doing to squeeze into it.'

'Not at all, Bronagh, and I've told you to call me Polly.' To her surprise, Bronagh crooked her arm. She slipped hers through the receptionist's rather liking the chumminess of the gesture.

''Tis hard to change the habit of a lifetime, Polly,' Bronagh said, and when they reached the other side of the road, she came to a standstill. 'Would you smell that air. Now that should be bottled, so it should.'

A car backfired, sending out a cloud of grimy, black smoke.

'Not that obviously,' Bronagh elaborated, flapping her hand. 'I meant the sea air. It's got to be good for you.'

'I know what you mean,' Polly said, having a good sniff so that the pair of them looked like they were bloodhounds tasked with tracking a scent. 'The smell of the seaside always gives me a yearning for fish and chips or an ice cream at the very least,' she continued. Both were a step up from the soggy potted meat sandwich picnics at the beach on the rare occasions their mammy had whisked her and her siblings off on the bus for a day at the seaside when she was a youngster. Somehow, none of them had minded the sprinkling of sand they'd wind up eating as well because something about sitting on the shore made them taste absolutely delicious. Nostalgia for those days when pleasures were simple and few, and treasured even more for being so, made her swallow hard.

'You're right. It does.'

They carried on. Polly was unaware they were strutting rather than walking in their Bendy Yoga Ladies jackets, both women oblivious to the bemused glances of Saturday morning shoppers. If a wind machine blew their hair back, they could have been starring in a music video.

'We could, you know?' Bronagh ventured as they reached the top of the lane where a pavement sign advertised this was where they'd find the Bendy Yoga Studio.

'What?'

'Buy ourselves a nice piece of battered fish and a scoop of chips and sit down on the pier after our workout. That yellow thing in the sky might not put out much heat, but it's doing its best.'

'And these jackets aren't just fashionable. They're toasty, warm. Maureen has such good taste.'

'She does that, and they are Polly.'

'I dare say we'll have earned ourselves a treat later, what with all the bending and twisting we're in for.'

'I dare say we will have.'

The two women, co-conspirators in pink jackets, smiled at each other before making their way to Roisin's studio.

Roisin greeted them warmly and told them to choose a mat. Polly and Bronagh scanned the studio, where five others sat on their mats.

'I'm worried if I get down on one of those there, I'll never get up again,' Polly said quietly to Bronagh, pointing to a pink mat at the back of the studio.

'Don't be.' A woman with a sensible, silver haircut said. 'We're all in the same boat. Aren't we girls?'

There was a murmured consensus.

'I'll give you a helping hand back up if you do the same for me.' The woman added, 'I'm Deirdre, by the way.'

'That sounds like a grand plan, Deirdre, and I'm Polly. This is my friend Bronagh.'

And just like that, Polly and Bronagh felt right at home.

'I think that's after going very well,' Bronagh said an hour and ten minutes later. 'You know what they say about no pain, no gain, and I can certainly feel my cord.' She patted her middle.

'I think it was core. You know, like an apple core, Rosi was on about. Can you believe she had us trying to touch our toes? And there was an awful lot of clenching things.'

'There was. I'd things squeezed. I didn't even know you could squeeze.'

Polly agreed. 'Although a few women there could have done with squeezing certain things as a preventive measure, if you catch my drift.'

'I do indeed, and I think we chose our mats wisely positioned over there by that scented thing Rosi has wafting about the place. At one point, the studio was windier than the windy city itself.'

'Chicago,' Polly supplied.

'No, the other one.'

Polly had no clue what the other one might be, but they left it at that as they swaggered cowgirl style on account of the Goddess squats they were after doing at yoga toward the fish and chip shop.

'And do you think those stretches for the hands Roisin had us doing helped your fingers like?'

Polly was taken aback. She wasn't aware Bronagh had noticed them. Her hands and the pain in her joints were hers and John Jospeh's little secret, or so she'd thought.

'I could see they were paining you when you were driving like.'

Polly supposed her knobbly finger joints were hard to miss as she unconsciously squeezed her hands inside her jacket pockets. It dawned on her doing so that the pain had eased. She pulled her hands from her pockets and opened them, wiggling her fingers. There was no doubt the stiffness and ever-present burning had eased between arriving at the Bendy Yoga Studio and leaving it. Whatever Rosi was after doing was pure magic, plain and simple. There was wonder in her voice when she spoke up, 'Do you know Bronagh, they did.'

'Will you go back next week then?' Bronagh asked, opening the door to the fish and chip shop.

'I think I will, yes. Will you?' Polly said, closing it behind them as they were enveloped in the smell of deep-frying food.

'That's good news because I'm enjoying myself, and you and I could make this a regular Saturday morning thing.'

Polly felt a warming in the part of her middle Rosi had referred to as her core; it spread past her ribs and into her chest, travelling up into her throat until it reached her mouth. Her lips curved into a bright smile back at Bronagh. The feeling was pleasure because she was enjoying herself too. 'I'd like that Bronagh. I'd like that very much.'

Chapter Twenty-eight

♥

'Oh, I've loads to tell you this morning,' Polly told the little red fox. Watching him snuffle across the courtyard, she was buoyed to see he'd lost that hungry manginess; his coat was richer, his tail full. The limp was improving each time she saw him. We all need something, Polly thought. Take herself, for instance. She'd needed a neutral confidante, while her foxy friend there had needed food. She liked to think they both needed company.

'Something magical is after happening this weekend. Not the pull a rabbit out of a hat sort of magic, and it's hard to explain what it is, but I suppose it's like I've been wearing this weighty cloak around my shoulders, and I'm after tossing it off.'

The food she'd laid out for him this morning was a piled-up feast. Mrs Baicu remembered to keep the weekend leftovers for Polly's grandson's imaginary pig, Padraig. The guests who'd made their way downstairs to the dining room can't have been a very hungry lot given how much had been scraped off their plates and into the container, she thought. Secretly, Polly liked to think it was because Mrs Baicu's full Irish paled compared to her own. Still and all, the woman was after doing her a good turn, and so come Friday, she'd leave her a jar of her homemade pickle and a note to say it was best enjoyed with cold meat or a slice of cheddar by way of a thank you.

The fox's eyes glowed bluish green caught in the sensor light he'd tripped as he stopped and fixed his gaze on Polly. The pearls of winter's morning mist danced in the yellow beam as Polly eyed him back. It was a wondrous thing how his eyes changed colour because most of the time they were amber, but when the light hit his iris at a certain angle like it was doing now, they changed to the colour of the sea in Howth harbour on Saturday. She clucked her tongue. 'Don't be worrying about me, you'll be hungry so. Tuck in.' Then she added, 'Bon Appétit,' just like Julia Childs.

The fox didn't need to be told twice.

Polly rested against the door frame, watching him gobble the food. Was there any point in telling him to slow down, or he'd give himself a tummy ache. A sentiment she'd send across the dinner table to her boys when they were hungry teenagers shovelling food in like there was no tomorrow. Probably not, she decided. Instead, she mentioned having gone to the yoga class with Bronagh and how, to her amazement, Roisin's hand exercises were helping with the pain in her fingers.

'I practised them at home on Sunday, and sure look, I can even do them here talking to you now.' She demonstrated and was gratified to see the fox look up from the sausage he was enjoying. As he watched her drop each finger down one by one, she saw his eyes had changed back to amber. 'I don't mind telling you either. John Joseph was very impressed with my forward bend. I told him to watch this space because I'd be touching my toes in no time. And did you know that balance when you stand on one leg and pretend to be a tree is very good for your brain? Who'd have thought?' Polly shook her head. 'She knows her stuff does, Rosi.'

There was no reply, of course, but then she'd not expected one because while she might enjoy her morning conversations with O'Mara's foxy visitor, they were always destined to be one-sided. Polly was stubborn, stoic, and prone to using bad language, but she wasn't doolally. Nor, she realised with a start, was she lonely. Not anymore. And, after a pause, she continued to tell her pointy-eared friend about her and Bronagh's lunch on the pier.

'I've known Bronagh Hanrahan for many years. More than I can count, but it dawned on me as we enjoyed our fish and chips, and very nice they were too, that I didn't know her. Not really. Sure, we know enough about each other's family to ask after them on a Monday morning, but we don't know what friends know about one another. The things you carry in here.' Polly laid her hand on her heart for a moment. 'But I think we put paid to that sitting on the pier in our pink jackets. I think I made a new friend on Saturday afternoon.'

Polly got that warm feeling again. It spread up from the pit of her stomach and ended with a smile as she chattered on.

'I'm sure Bronagh won't mind me sharing our little chat with you because it's not like it will go any further. Not unless you were to meet up with Doctor fecking Doolittle over there in the Iveagh gardens.' Polly laughed at her little joke, and as the fox made short work of half a sausage, she lowered her voice in case the walls had ears.

'She's finding it terribly hard to say goodbye to her Lennie each time he returns to Liverpool. The pair of them were after having a grand time in Santorini together, and she'd hoped he might announce his intentions to move back to Dublin then, but he didn't. I suggested she tell him how she feels, but Bronagh doesn't think it would be fair, not if she couldn't do the same for him and move to Liverpool. She can't, of course. There's her mam, for one thing. She's poorly, and Bronagh's looked after her for years. Then there's O'Mara's. To leave the guesthouse would be like leaving her family.'

Polly thought about how Bronagh had mentioned Leonard's sister Joan, with whom she'd grown close, and how she called in on her once a week for tea and cake. She'd invited Polly to join her this week, saying she and Joan would get along very well. Polly was looking forward to it. Joan was of a mind to tick her brother off on his next visit and tell him he'd a good woman in Bronagh, and it was high time he moved back to Ireland because life was too short for faffing about like so. Then she thought about how Bronagh had listened, head tilted to one side as she nibbled her chips, about the arthritis in her hands and how it worried her that she'd have to give up her job at O'Mara's if it got worse. 'That would break my heart, so it would,' Polly repeated to the fox what she'd said to Bronagh.

They'd laughed too when Polly talked about John Joseph and his well-meant but eejitty remarks about her taking up craft work of some description. Bronagh had wiped her eyes with the back of her hands and said she could just see her sitting at a table with a group of genteel crafting women carrying on about the embroidery silk not fitting through the fecking needle.

'Bronagh says I need to see Doctor Barry because there's bound to be something that will help with the arthritis. And that it's not nothing, and I won't be wasting his time. I promised to ring him this morning, and she said she'd check that I'd made an appointment before I left for home. I'm going to phone Roisin too and tell her those hand exercises she was after doing with us on Saturday helped me. I'll ask her if there's more she can show me. Bronagh said I need to help myself, and she's right, so I'm going to leave you now because I've plenty to be getting on with.'

The fox glanced up at her, and this time, his eyes were the colour of the sea.

Chapter

Twenty-nine

♥

Roisin wasn't surprised when Mrs Flaherty telephoned her on Monday afternoon. Bronagh had already given her the heads up about what had been on O'Mara's breakfast cook's mind of late. The mystery had been solved. Although, she'd had to ask Bronagh to repeat herself because she'd been talking with her mouthful. Guessing as to what Bronagh was munching on at the other end of the line, had given Roisin a hankering for custard creams, followed by a trip downstairs to the basement kitchen of O'Mara's in the hope of one of Mrs Flaherty's rasher sandwiches. She'd had to content herself with the apple she'd brought to the studio, but it wasn't the same.

So it was, she was prepared when she picked up the phone at the Bendy Yoga Studio with twenty minutes to spare until her next class to hear Mrs Flaherty's voice. She'd done her best to sound like her call was unexpected, getting the conversation underway by asking her how she'd enjoyed Saturday's class. Hearing Mrs Flaherty say she'd enjoyed it very much and that she and Bronagh were looking forward to making yoga and lunch a regular weekend get-together made Roisin happy. If she could convert those two into seeing the benefits of yoga, the world would be her oyster! Then, realising that it sounded like she was a religious leader seeking world domination, Roisin re-focussed on the point of the call. 'Was there anything you'd like to work on next Saturday, Mrs Flaherty?'

The ball was in Mrs Flaherty's court, and she'd confessed the arthritis in her hands was beginning to make her life a misery. 'Those hand exercises you did toward the end of the class were helpful, Rosi. I was wondering if you'd more up your sleeve?'

'I'm thrilled to hear they helped Mrs Flaherty, and I'd love to show you a few more exercises.' Deciding to strike while the iron was hot, Roisin added, 'I've a window tomorrow afternoon between two and three if you're free to call up to the studio?'

'I could do that, and it's very good of you to fit me in like so, Rosi.'

'You always found time to listen to me, Mrs Flaherty. I'd like to help.'

Now, she tidied the studio between classes, waiting for her favourite cook. She didn't have to wait long.

'It's only me, Rosi,' a familiar voice called up the stairs.

'Come on up, Mrs Flaherty.' Roisin called back, rolling up the straps used in the last class for the leg stretches. She heard the door below bang shut and plodding footfall on the stairs, and then the breakfast cook appeared, a little out of breath at the entrance. Roisin didn't do a double take this time because she was slowly getting used to seeing Mrs Flaherty outside of O'Mara's in the apron she seemingly always had on. She'd come prepared for whatever Roisin would show her by wearing her pink jacket and leggings with an oversized tee shirt overtop. Roisin wondered if the shirt was pilfered from Mr Flaherty's drawers. The apples of her cheeks were rosier than usual, she noticed, which was probably down to the cold, and she was quick to remove her jacket as the warmth of the studio hit her.

Roisin put the folded strap down on the yoga blocks at the foot of the mat and took Mrs Flaherty's jacket from her. She hung it on the hooks Donal had put on the wall in the narrow hallway between the studio and the bathroom. Then greeted Mrs Flaherty properly with a hug. She gave good cuddles, did Mrs Flaherty Roisin thought, burrowing in. It had something to do with having big bosoms because Aisling was a good cuddler, too.

'Was it a busy morning for you at O'Mara's?' Roisin asked as they parted.

'It was. We'd a load of businessmen staying. They always like a hearty breakfast to see them through all those important meetings they're in Dublin for. Oh, and there was an annoying woman from somewhere in Canada with a list of food allergies longer than my arm. No eggs, no dairy, no gluten. In the end, all she could eat was a banana. A fecking banana. What sort of breakfast is that?' Polly shook her head in disgust.

Roisin grinned because this was the woman she knew and loved.

Mrs Flaherty moved on from annoyance over the yellow fruit to say, 'I appreciate you squeezing me in like Roisin. You're a busy girl these days.'

Only her mammy, Bronagh, and Mrs Flaherty referred to her as a girl. It made her smile. 'I am and love it, but I'm never too busy for you, Mrs Flaherty. Sure, how often did I give you earache as a child?'

'Not once, Rosi. I loved having you join me in the kitchen. I'm looking forward to the toddler Kiera getting a little bigger and popping down of her own accord to see me.'

'And I think, like me, she'll find there's a magic ingredient to make you feel instantly better in those rasher sandwiches of yours when she does.'

'Well then, we're even with this magic business, Rosi, because I'm after thinking there's magic properties in those mats of yours.' She pointed to where they were neatly spaced out in three rows.

'Come on then. Let's see if that's true.' Roisin sank cross-legged on her teacher's mat positioned at the front of the studio. At the same time, Polly, wary of whether she'd get up again, settled on the mat in front of her. Now, she'd have liked to emulate Roisin's cross-legged position, but while the mind was willing, her body was not, and her legs remained splayed out in front of her. She followed Roisin's lead as they raised their arms skyward, inhaling and exhaling several times. An audible click of body parts sounded, and Polly felt her neck muscles crunching in a good way when Roisin moved on to doing some head rolls.

Polly hoped the smile she had on her face was beatific like Roisin's.

'Now we're going to remove the flesh from our sit bones and fix them into the ground.'

'Excuse me, Rosi.' Polly didn't like interrupting the flow of things, but she needed to be clear about what she was about to fix into the ground. 'I didn't like to ask on Saturday, but by sit bones, do you mean arse?'

An un-yoga-like snort escaped from Roisin. 'I do, Mrs Flaherty.'

'Grand.' She gave Roisin a thumbs up and wriggled about on her mat, ensuring her arse was screwed onto the mat. 'I'm good to go now.'

'Now we'll draw ourselves up tall so our spines are nice and straight. Imagine you've a piece of string attached to the top of your head.' Roisin pretended to pull an invisible piece of string up to demonstrate.

'Like a puppet?'

'Exactly.'

Mrs Flaherty shot up several centimetres in height.

Twenty minutes later, Polly was staring at her hands in wonder. 'Magic is what it is, Rosi. Magic.'

Roisin smiled. Moments like this made yoga magical for her. 'And, you're going to see your Doctor as well?'

'How did you know that?' Mrs Flaherty looked up from her hands, frowning.

Whoops, Roisin thought quickly, not wanting to land Bronagh in it. 'I'm assuming is all. You should because I'm sure something can be prescribed to help.'

'I am, as it happens, although I was reluctant to make an appointment.'

'Why?' Roisin stayed where she was still cross-legged on her mat.

'It's the march of time responsible for these aches and pains, Rosi. They're part of the cycle of life. Sure, my dear mammy suffered from arthritis and just had to get on with it. Besides, there are people out there far worse off than me with my moans and groans, needing to see him. I didn't like to take up his time.'

Roisin's top knot wobbled indignantly. 'Mrs Flaherty, you're as important as anyone else, and if you've been in pain, then you're in need.' The blissful smile had been replaced by a frown. 'It's a mam thing this not wanting to bother others when we need help.'

'What do you mean, Rosi?' Mrs Flaherty picked a piece of fluff off her leggings content to stay put on her mat for as long as possible.

'I mean, once we become mam's, we start putting our needs last, and sometimes it's to our detriment because if it catches up on us and we lose our health, it means we stop being able to help those we love.'

Mrs Flaherty rolled this about in her head. If she didn't help herself with her hands, she'd be in too much pain to work. It might mean handing her notice in at O'Mara's. The driving would have to go, too. Something else occurred to her. What about picking up her smallest grandbaby? Would she no longer be able to do that? Her world suddenly began to shrink wrap around her, and for a moment, she couldn't breathe. Then, realising Roisin's lips were moving, she concentrated on what she was saying.

'You are important,' Roisin was repeating. 'You've a family who needs you, Mrs Flaherty, and O'Mara's would be lost without you.'

Polly was nodding. Roisin had her attention.

'So, reframe the way you've been thinking. Your health has to be at the top of your list of priorities because you'd be letting yourself and others down by ignoring it.'

There was a saying about light bulb moments, Polly thought. This was one of those. Rosi was right. 'Bronagh convinced me I should make an appointment to see Doctor Barry. I'm off to see him Thursday afternoon.' That was a step in the right direction, and so was coming to see Rosi today.

'That's good. You're taking positive action. Between whatever your doctor prescribes for you and practising those exercises we did together regularly, you'll feel like a different woman in no time.' Roisin thought there was everything to be gained from being positive in life and nothing at all to be had from negativity.

'Well, I'll certainly be doing the exercises, and we'll wait and see what the good doctor has to say. I don't want to feel like a different woman, though, Rosi. I want to feel like a better version of the old one.'

'And you will,' Roisin said, staying with the positivity theme.

'That's more than enough about me. What about you? I've not had a proper chance to catch up with you and find out how you're getting on with that young man of yours or how Noah's liking his new school?'

Roisin's ear-to-ear smile said it all. 'Shay and I are very happy. He's brilliant with Noah, too, and they adore each other. Noah's even growing his hair like Shay's, although that's not good because we had a notice from school saying the nits are doing the rounds. I'd rather he kept it short.'

'He's happy, Rosi, that's the important thing. And, if he does get the nits, don't be faffing with all that natural shite. It's the chemical warfare you need to take the little buggers out. Take it from someone who's been there and done that.'

'Hopefully, I don't have to go there.' Roisin shuddered at the thought of the parasites jumping about her son's scalp.

'And school, the nits aside, how's Noah finding it?'

'He's loving it now. We had a few hiccups at the start. They weren't down to him not settling in so much but more being the creator of a new, popular game that took the school by storm; Sexed.'

'I beg your pardon?'

'You heard right. It's a long story about Mammy's dog Pooh's inappropriate behaviour around a cockapoo. It saw Noah come up with a new and improved, in his opinion, game of tag.'

'Sexed?'

Roisin nodded, her expression grim, and Polly burst out laughing. 'Bless his heart.'

'That's not what the other parents said, but I think things will settle down from hereon in because the novelty of the new game's wearing off.'

'It does after a while,' Mrs Flaherty said.

Roisin wasn't sure whether they were still discussing the game, but she wasn't about to go there. 'He's made friends with a group of kids and thinks Miss Dunlop, his teacher, can do no wrong.'

'And, what about his father?'

'Noah's had so much upheaval in his little life, what with me and his dad splitting up, Colin leaving for the Emirates, and us setting up home in Ireland with Shay. His dad telephones him twice weekly, telling him stories about his life over there. At first, I thought those calls made things worse because Noah always played up in the days after. They don't seem to affect him as much now he's busy with school and friends. He'll see him over the holidays because Colin's home for Christmas. We've not worked out the finer points of that yet.'

'Children are resilient, Rosi.'

Roisin nodded. She was very proud of Noah.

'And there's no other news you want to tell me?' Polly looked pointedly at Roisin's tummy, which was as flat as a pancake.

Rosi wrapped her hands self-consciously around her middle. 'No!'

'And how are you managing the studio with Maureen being away?' Polly moved on.

Roisin hesitated. Mrs Flaherty and her mammy were fond of one another. There was nothing to be gained from complaining. She needed to practice what she preached, she thought, running through her positivity versus negativity mantra.

Polly picked up on the hesitation. 'What's on your mind, Rosi?'

Nothing ever got past Mrs Flaherty, Roisin thought, wishing she'd bought a frying pan, a packet of bacon and a loaf of bread with her. Oh, and sauce. She liked plenty of red sauce on her rasher sandwich.

'Whatever it is will go no further, and I might be able to help. You won't know unless you try me,' Polly cajoled.

'I don't want to moan because that's what it will sound like.'

'Rosi O'Mara, who was after telling me about how us mams need to look after ourselves more just now?'

'I'm not sick, though.'

'Keeping things locked up inside is a surefire way to make yourself sick, though. Out with it.'

Roisin's face crumpled as she opened up, feeling like a teenager again, offloading her latest drama. She spoke about how important the studio was to her because it symbolised so much more than a place to teach yoga. Pausing only to search for the words to explain how it was her opportunity to finally achieve something concrete. 'I wanted to show everyone I could set my mind to something and stick with it.'

Mrs Flaherty didn't interrupt. Not once waiting until she'd finished before speaking up. 'Rosi, you don't want to spend your life feeling like you need to prove yourself to others.'

'I mostly wanted to prove it to myself.'

'And you have. Sure, look around you.'

Roisin shook her head, that dark bun on top of her head wobbling once more. 'But I've not done it on my own. I took the easy way out by accepting Mammy's help financially. Then she decided that made us partners, and somewhere along the way, it stopped being my studio and became hers too.' She studied her nails, cut sensibly short.

'Ah, Rosi. That's something else we mammies are prone to do. Taking over, interfering, and having too much to say about what our children are doing. We can't help it, you see. You'll find out for yourself when Noah's older. And what it boils down to is fear that our children don't need us anymore.'

Rosi looked up through teary eyes. 'But I'll always need my mam.'

'I know, but she probably needs to hear it from you. It might help her step back from the studio and leave you to get on with things.'

'She's a vested interest in this place too, though.' Roisin shrugged, 'I can't very well tell her I need her in my life. Of course, I do, but she's to back off and leave me to my business.'

'No Rosi. That's not what I'm suggesting. Your mam has a good head for figures, doesn't she?'

'She does,' Roisin agreed. Years of running O'Mara's had honed her ability to keep accounts. 'I hate bookwork personally. The maths gene bypassed me.'

'Then why don't you suggest she takes over doing your books? Delegate. Offload the things you're not keen on and give yourself more time to focus on what you do well.'

Roisin looked up from her intense thumbnail study, curious to hear the rest of Polly's words.

'If you ask her to do, say, the bookwork for starters, and stress how important it is and how you just can't wrap your head around that side of things. Play on how much the thought of it stresses you out and how much easier it would make your life if she were to take it over.'

'I see where you're going with this now.'

'That way, she still has a finger in the pie, and not only feels like she's being useful, but she is being a help to you.'

'I could suggest she do the books at home so that the class noise doesn't distract her because she'll need to concentrate.'

'Now you're cooking with gas, Roisin.'

Roisin suddenly lunged forward, nearly knocking Polly backwards as she flung her arms around her and said, 'And, don't ever forget, I'll always need you too, Mrs Flaherty.'

Chapter Thirty

♥

The handle of Pooh's lead was wrapped twice around Roisin's hand as she stood chatting to Becca outside the primary school. It felt like overkill, given he was sitting sedately by her feet, but she didn't trust him. The minute she relaxed her grip, some good-looking girl dog would give him the glad eye, and he'd be off! He looked dapper today in the red jacket Mammy insisted he wore on days when there was a chance of the ground freezing. Today was precisely that sort of a day. She saw two older children pretending to smoke, exhaling a cloud of white into the frigid air as they sauntered in through the gates. She and Becca were making the most of a few minutes catching up before duty called, even though it was too cold to be standing about. Becca had told Roisin how much she'd enjoyed the yoga class she'd attended and how a couple of women from the medical practice where she worked were interested in coming along to check it out for themselves. Then, they'd moved on to discussing their plans for Christmas. It was still well over a month away, but both women knew the weeks would fly by in a flash between now and then.

'Have you decided about Noah spending Christmas with his Granny and dad in London?'

'I have, as it happens. I asked Noah what he wanted to do, and he said he wants to spend it here with me and Shay and the rest of the family this year, but maybe next year he'll go to London.'

'How did that go down?'

Roisin recalled her conversation with Colin and Elsa, his mother. They didn't argue much, not when she told them it was Noah's decision. 'Surprisingly okay. He leaves the day after Boxing Day to stay with his Granny and Colin for five days.'

'While the cats away and all that.' Becca gave a lurid wink.

Roisin laughed.

'And what about your brother and his wife? Have they named their baby yet?' Becca asked, stamping her feet, trying to stop them from going numb.

'No. We're still stuck with the 'babby,'' Roisin, huddled inside her pink jacket.

'How much longer are your Mam and Donal staying on in LA?'

'They're back tomorrow, as it happens. I'm picking them up from the airport after my last class in the afternoon.'

Becca looked wistful. 'Palm trees and sunshine. I hope they had a good holiday.'

'I don't know about a holiday. They'll need one when they get home,' Roisin laughed. 'I think Patrick's had Mammy run off her feet.'

'And how do you feel about her being back on board at the studio?'

Roisin had already told Becca how much she'd enjoyed having sole charge this week. 'Actually,' she replied with a twinkle in her eyes. 'I've got a plan where my mammy is concerned.'

'Ooh, do tell.'

'Well, it started with a heart-to-heart with Mrs Flaherty. She's the breakfast cook at O'Mara's. I love her to bits. She's always been a good listener.' Roisin relayed her suggestion about tasking Maureen with the all-important accounts.

Becca gave a slow nod. 'That could work.'

'It better.'

'She sounds like a smart woman, your Mrs Flaherty. Maybe I'll have a word with my mammy and tell her how much I need her and see if she butts out of my private life. Not that there's much for her to be butting out of.'

Roisin grinned. 'Good luck with that. Mrs Flaherty is a very wise woman. You'd want to try one of her rasher sandwiches. They're the best.'

'Now you're making me hungry, and it's hours until morning tea!'

'Sorry! I haven't forgotten our night out at Quinn's either. We'll touch base on that next week shall we?'

'I'm looking forward to it.'

A flash of something bright caught Roisin's eye. 'Oh look, there's Philomena.' She was hard to miss in that coat of hers. Mind you, she wasn't in a position to talk. Nobody would call her a wallflower in her Bendy Yoga Ladies jacket. 'Is that a neck brace she's after wearing?'

'Who cares?' Becca shrugged.

'I shouldn't but... Becca, would you hold Pooh for a few ticks?'

'What are you going to say to her?' Becca took the lead, but Roisin was already picking her way over the icy tarmac. 'You already apologised when you'd nothing to apologise for! Look where that got you.'

Philomena was waving the last of her von Trapp children off when Roisin reached her and heard her shout after them. 'And remember, no playing that game!' she thought about turning back. Instead, she tugged up her imaginary big girl pants and stood her ground.

'Good morning, Philomena. How're you doing?' Did she smell? Roisin wondered as the other woman took a step back from her. If she had a cross and garlic bulbs, she'd no doubt shake them at her.

Once she'd regained her composure, Philomena's expression closed like the shutters had been pulled down. She bent and scooped Nancy up. It looked awkward, given the brace around her neck. As for the little cockapoo, she wasn't happy. She wriggled and squirmed because she'd seen Pooh regal in his red coat.

As for Pooh, he'd seen Nancy and was frisking about while Becca looked like she was trying to keep hold of a bucking bronco. The poodle and the cockapoo were star-crossed lovers, and she decided she'd better keep this short so they could go their separate ways. She looked to Philomena expectantly, waiting for a reply to her question.

'I'm fine, thank you. Was there something you were after?'

'I noticed your neck brace.' You couldn't very well miss it. 'I wanted to check you were okay?' Roisin wasn't sure what response she'd get and was prepared for her to repeat that she was fine and get on her way.

'It's an old whiplash injury from a car accident, and it always aches when it's cold like this.'

Roisin spoke without thinking, 'I could help you manage the pain with some exercises if you wanted to come to a class at the Bendy Yoga Ladies studio.'

Suspicion flickered in Philomena's eyes as she raked Roisin's face, trying to gauge her motive.

'Listen, Philomena, all I'm trying to do with my studio is help people, and I'd like to see if I can help you. Why don't you come and have a complimentary class to see if the exercises I can show you ease that aching. Think of it as an early Christmas gift. You've nothing to lose.'

Philomomena flushed the same colour as Roisin's jacket, but whether it was from a guilty conscience, Roisin couldn't tell. The woman was clearly flustered.

'We'll see.' Was all she said as she turned away.

Roisin returned to Becca and relieved her of Pooh duty.

Becca did a few shoulder rolls. 'He's strong. I only just managed to keep hold of him.'

'Yeah, sorry about that.'

'How did it go anyway?' Becca gave a nod in Philomena's direction. She was making her way, still with a firm hold of Nancy, toward her Land Rover.

'I offered her a complimentary class to see if it helped with her neck.'

'And what did she say?'

'We'll see.'

'Rude cow. You're too nice, Roisin. I don't know why you bothered.'

'Because I'm doing things my way, Becca. Whether or not she takes me up on the offer doesn't matter. I know I've done what feels right and been the bigger person.'

'Like I said, you're too nice, but that's okay. I like you anyway.'

Roisin smiled at that, and then Becca glanced at her watch. 'Crap! I'd better get a wriggle on. Catch you later.'

'See you,' Roisin called. 'Come on, Pooh. You're off to see Aunty Rosemary and Uncle Cathal Carrick the Cobbler now.'

Her step as she set off felt lighter. Regardless of whether Philomena showed up at a class, there'd be no more petty underhandedness from her. She was sure of that. One down, one to go, Roisin thought, because Mammy was home tomorrow. 'Wish me luck, Pooh.'

There was no reply. Pooh was sulking.

Chapter Thirty-one

'Brianna Buttercup O'Mara,' Maureen announced the minute she burst through Customs into the Arrivals Hall of Dublin Airport. Donal, pushing the trolley, was bringing up the rear while a woman trotting alongside him, clutching a pen, flapped a piece of paper. All the O'Mara family were used to Donal continuously being mistaken for the country music legend he paid tribute to with The Gamblers. Getting accosted for autographs happened, and Donal took it in his stride. He was always polite. This time, however, Roisin could see he looked frazzled and fed up as he gave the woman short shrift. Your woman was obviously a fan because she wasn't taking the hint.

Maureen threw herself at Roisin, who managed to stay upright and see over her mammy's shoulder that the easy-going, nothing phased him, Donal had just run over the woman's foot with the trolley!

'I'll sue. I don't care if you are Kenny Rogers!' The woman had dropped her pen and paper and was dancing about, clutching her foot.

'I'm not fecking Kenny Rogers. I'm Donal McCarthy from Howth.'

Best they make a speedy exit, Roisin thought.

'Tis good to be back on Irish soil. Although I feel badly for abandoning Patrick. He's finding fatherhood a big adjustment. But Donal and I are in need of sleep.'

'I can see that Mammy.' Roisin kept away from the trolley as she greeted Donal with a cautious welcome home hug. Then, seeing the Kenny fan hobbling toward a security guard, she herded them out of the building and into their car.

Roisin did her best to tune her mammy out as she exited the car parking building and left the airport behind, although she was interested in hearing they'd caught up with Bobby-Jean while they were there. She was a terrible backseat driver even though she was sitting in the passenger seat. Donal's head was lolling, and he jerked himself awake with random little snores, Roisin saw with a glimpse in the rearview mirror.

'Anyway, Rosi, I've decided I'll cough loudly when Father Fitzpatrick gets to the Buttercup bit during the christening,' Maureen said.

'They're going to have her christened here, then?'

'They will be if I've anything to do with it.'

Brianna. Roisin tried her little niece's name on for size. It was pretty. She liked it and thought they should all count their blessings that Buttercup had been relegated to second place. By all accounts, Brianna O'Mara was keeping her parents on their toes already, she thought, remembering what it was like suddenly being responsible for this tiny person who needed you for absolutely everything.

'At least Patrick slept right through the other night.'

Roisin pretended she hadn't heard that as she pointedly asked after Cindy.

'Oh, she's a grand little Mammy. Although I had to show her how to wrap the babby Brianna so her wee hands don't flail about when she's asleep and wake her up.'

Roisin listened as Mammy continued to relay the list of things she'd had to show Cindy over the week and smiled to herself. She also had a mammy-in-law who'd shown her the 'right' way to do everything when Noah was born. Colin's mam had been a right royal pain in the arse, but she'd known it came from a place of love for her new grandson, as would Cindy with Mammy.

'And Pooh? How's he been?'

'Grand Mammy. He's had a great time with Rosemary and Cathal when I've been busy at the studio, and Noah's loved having him stay.' She decided not to mention the touch-and-go incident where Pooh had been under suspicion for eating Mr Nibbles. All's well that ended well. 'I almost forgot. Have a look inside the glove box. I picked up the copy of Howth Happenings. It was delivered this morning, but I've not had a chance to flick through it.'

Maureen located it and began to eagerly leaf through it in search of the social pages.

'Hurry up, Mammy. I hope your Ger Collins man is after taking a few decent shots.'

There was a sharp gasp of breath from the passenger seat.

'What is it, Mammy?'

'Oh, it's a good shot of us alright, Roisin.' Maureen flapped the folded back page in Roisin's direction.

Roisin risked a quick glance to see herself and Mammy matching in wintergreen. She looked surprised, and Mammy looked like a pufferfish. So he'd opted not to use the one he'd taken of her alone, Roisin thought, drumming the steering wheel. 'What about the other photographs? Give us a look, Mammy.'

'Not while you're after driving Roisin.'

This didn't bode well, and as soon as she could, Roisin indicated and pulled over. She held her hand out for the magazine, which was handed over reluctantly. Then, flicking through to the right page, she screamed.

Donal instantly blinked his eyes open, murmuring, 'There, there, Babby Buttercup.'

'Brianna,' Maureen lobbed over her shoulder.

Roisin took a second, slower look at the horror frozen in time on the pages of Howth Happenings underneath a passable snap of her sisters, Bronagh and Mrs Flaherty. Bold Brenda had been captured, demonstrating a downward-facing dog for the camera. Roisin had to turn the magazine upside down to confirm this, and there was no doubt. It was Brenda.

'She looks like a geriatric porn star,' Roisin wailed.

'No. Not at all.' Maureen attempted to soothe her. 'She looks flexible, is all.'

Roisin ran through her pranayama, breathing at Mammy's insistence before driving off.

As they reached the landmarks, signalling they were nearly home, Maureen asked, 'Has there been any more of that nonsense from your cockapoo woman. Because I'll tell her what I think of her shenanigans with that letter, so I will.'

Roisin gripped the steering wheel a little tighter because this was her moment. She forgot all about Bold Brenda and went for it. 'It's all sorted, Mammy. You've no need to be worrying yourself about that.'

'And you Roisin? How have you coped on your own like? I know you said you were fine managing the studio, but I know what you girls are like, and I worried that you might be trying not to worry me.'

The irony of her comment went over the top of her head, and Roisin said, 'I missed you.'

Now, that was music to Maureen's ears, and she sat up a little straighter in her seat. 'Well, I missed you too, Rosi and your sisters, your menfolk, the babbies, and the toddler Kiera, Noah and Pooh. But you know Patrick and Cindy needed me too, and sometimes you've got to share.'

Jaysus wept. Roisin recalled Mammy imparting a similar sentiment over toys when they were children.

'And the babby, Brianna needed me, too.'

'Of course she did, Mammy. But I was thinking about things while you were away.'

'Oh yes?' Maureen's eyes, bloodshot and baggy from a week's worth of broken sleep, were also suspicious.

'I couldn't have got the studio up and running without you. I realise I've not told you how grateful I am for all your help.'

''Tis only what any good Mammy worth her salt would do, Roisin.'

'And I want you to know how much I need you.'

Maureen reached across and patted her daughter's leg. 'I know you do, pet.'

'I'll always need my Mammy.'

'Yes, yes. Of course you will.'

'And I really need you to do something for me.'

'What would that be, Rosi?'

Roisin could see she had Mammy eating out the palm of her hand. 'The bookwork for the studio. You know the accounts like? I've no head for sums.'

'I remember. Your maths teacher told me and your dear late daddy there was no hope.'

'Yes, well then, you know what I'm saying. I can't make anything add up. It would help me so much, and I'd sleep better at night knowing the business's financials were in your safe, capable hands.' Roisin worried she'd laid it on too thick, but then, with a sideways glance, she saw the gleam in her mammy's eyes.

'The bookwork, you say?'

'The bookwork Mammy.'

'And it would be a big help to you, like?'

'It would, but maybe it's asking too much? I know how busy you are.'

'I'm sure I could find a window of time to do it, Roisin.'

'Of course, it would be much easier if you did them at home because there's nowhere you could set yourself up at the studio. Not when you'd be needing to concentrate.'

Maureen nodded and agreed. Her mind, however, was racing on. 'Would I have a title like?'

'You would, Mammy.'

'And what would that be?'

'Chief Internal Accounting Officer. Ciao for short. Like the Italian greeting.'

'C.I.A.O., ciao. I like it. It's a catchy ring to it, so it does.'

Roisin wasn't surprised. She knew how much her mam loved a title, but she loved an abbreviation even more, and risking another glance at her, she saw her eyes were glazed over. She guessed, quite correctly, that her mammy had just drifted off into a fantasy where she was telling Rosemary Farrell and the line-dancing ladies how busy she was in her new role as CIAO of the Bendy Yoga Studio.

It made her smile, and she knew when she'd dropped Mammy and Donal safely home to be reunited with Pooh, she'd telephone Mrs Flaherty to thank her. Her suggestion had worked like magic.

One month later

♥

I t was Sunday morning, and Christmas was upon them. Down-stairs, Roisin could hear the clattering of Noah and Shay having breakfast while she was tapping her foot impatiently, sitting on the loo seat lid in the bathroom. She knew Noah would be telling Shay all about the Spiderman toys he'd requested in his letter to Santa, as he'd been doing every morning since the 1st of December. He would also, no doubt, be trying to con an extra chocolate from his advent calendar.

To while away the dragging seconds, she thought about the studio. It was fully booked most days now, something she attributed to word of mouth, the pink lady jackets, and Bold Brenda. The photograph featured in Howth Happenings had seen the Bendy Yoga Studio in-undated with calls from women of a certain vintage. It was a case of, 'I'll have what she's having.'

Bronagh and Mrs Flaherty were Saturday morning regulars and tootled off after class with a group of fellow yoga ladies for lunch. From what Mrs Flaherty had told her when she'd last asked how her hands were, the discomfort was much more manageable these days. Donal was embracing his weekly yoga classes in his tracksuit bottoms. As for Mammy, she thoroughly enjoyed her new role as CIAO of the

Bendy Yoga Studio. Roisin felt they'd found a happy balance where her input was concerned.

Life was good and Roisin knew she'd plenty of blessings to be counting. Her baby niece for one. The family would all gather soon in Dublin for the babby Brianna's christening, and Roisin couldn't wait to give her a cuddle.

Her eyes flitted to the bathroom vanity. Would it be ready yet? It must be time, she decided, getting off the loo, to pick up the test from where she'd left it to develop. Roisin squeezed her eyes shut. She was almost too scared to look.

'On the count of three, Rosi,' she whispered. 'One, two, three!'

Two pink lines! There were two pink lines. Roisin closed her eyes again and opened them to double-check before flinging open the bathroom door and hollering, 'Shay! Come here to me now. I've got something to tell you!'

THE END

Dear Reader,

Thank you so much for joining me for more shenanigans with the O'Mara family in "Mat Magic at O'Mara's." Your support and enthusiasm for the O'Mara family mean the world to me.

If this latest instalment made you smile, then that's my job done. I very much hope it did, and I would be immensely grateful if you could share these stories with your fellow readers. Recommending the books and leaving a review or starred rating on Amazon or Goodreads would be a fantastic way to help others discover the O'Mara family.

Your encouragement and feedback are invaluable, and I so appreciate your time spent with the O'Mara family xx Michelle.

Book 16 out 28 July, 2024!
Pre-order Available here: https://books2read.com/u/mg5dAR
Matchmaking at O'Mara's

In the heart of Dublin, at the iconic O'Mara's guesthouse overlooking St Stephen's Green, Bronagh Hanrahan has been presiding over reception for what seems like forever. Her romance with Leonard Walsh, once a guest himself, blossomed thanks to a gentle matchmaking nudge from the guesthouse's manager, Aisling O'Mara. Their romance has gone from strength to strength, but lately, a formidable obstacle has emerged – the Irish Sea.

Leonard, hailing from Liverpool, crosses the water regularly to be with Bronagh, and she's had enough of saying hello and goodbye. Caring for her elderly mother means Bronagh can't uproot her life in Dublin. Yet, Leonard has ties in Dublin with his sister Joan, who, like Bronagh, yearns for him to return to his roots and can't under his reluctance to do so.

Aisling decides to play Cupid again and steer the couple toward a more permanent arrangement when Leonard is back to attend an O'Mara family christening as Bronagh's guest. Little does Aisling know that Leonard harbours a secret in Liverpool. A secret that could change everything between him and Bronagh.

Also By Michelle Vernal

Novels

The Cooking School on the Bay

Second-hand Jane

Staying at Eleni's

The Traveller's Daughter

Sweet Home Summer

When We Say Goodbye

And...

Series fiction

<u>The Guesthouse on the Green Series</u>

Book 1 - O'Mara's

Book 2 – Moira-Lisa Smile

Book 3 – What goes on Tour

Book 4 – Rosi's Regrets

Book 5 – Christmas at O'Mara's

Book 6 – A Wedding at O'Mara's

Book 7 – Maureen's Song

Book 8 – The O'Maras in LaLa Land

Book 9 – Due in March

Book 10 – A Baby at O'Mara's

Book 11 – The Housewarming

Book 12 – Rainbows over O'Mara's

Book 13- An O'Maras Reunion

Book 14-The O'Maras Go Greek

Book 15 Mat Magic at O'Mara's

Book 16 Matchmaking at O'Mara's Pre-order here: https://books2rea d.com/u/mg5dAR

Liverpool Brides Series

The Autumn Posy

The Winter Posy

The Spring Posy

The Summer Posy

Isabel's Story

The Promise

The Letter

The Little Irish Village

Christmas in the Little Irish Village

New Beginnings in the Little Irish Village

A Christmas Miracle in the little Irish Village

About the Author

Michelle Vernal lives in Christchurch, New Zealand with her husband, two teenage sons and attention seeking tabby cats, Humphrey and Savannah. Before she started writing novels, she had a variety of jobs:

Pharmacy shop assistant, girl who sold dried up chips and sausages at a hot food stand in a British pub, girl who sold nuts (for 2 hours) on a British market stall, receptionist, P.A...Her favourite job though is the one she has now – writing stories she hopes leave her readers with a satisfied smile on their face.

Visit Michelle at www.michellevernalbooks.com to find out more about her books.

Printed in Great Britain
by Amazon